HEY

Also by Andrew Meehan

One Star Awake
The Mystery of Love
Instant Fires
Best Friends

HEY MAN

Andrew Meehan

MUSWELL
PRESS

First published by Muswell Press in 2026

Typeset in Bembo by M Rules
Printed by CPI Group (UK) Ltd, Croydon CR0 4YY

A CIP record for this book
is available from the British Library

ISBN: 9781919247106
eISBN: 97819247106

Our authorised representative in the EU for product safety
is Easy Access System Europe, Mustamäe tee 50,
10621 Tallinn, Estonia
gpsr.requests@easproject.com

Muswell Press, London N6 5HQ
www.muswell-press.co.uk

FSC www.fsc.org
MIX
Paper | Supporting responsible forestry
FSC® C013604

2 4 6 8 10 9 7 5 3 1

O men, how long will your hearts be closed?

PSALMS 4
(the *Hebrew Bible*, Grail translation)

You Know What

1989

You may know of Tommy Carmody. He was the type of person who stories attach themselves to.

I won't be able to cover the whole story here, but I hope I've been truthful about everything I remember. It's also true that I don't know how to talk about him without seeking his approval, which he's not here to offer, and which I might not get.

I was due to be his lodger for the summer, but it was weeks before we met. He was shooting a film in France—something to do with Gérard Depardieu and musketeers—and he'd mailed a key for his house in Crouch End to my dad, along with instructions that I was to let myself in and make myself at home, but not too much at home.

I was on my way to medical school, and Dad's diagnosis was that this man would be a good role model. His cousin, who was always in the mood for a party, and always slightly cross with himself about it, who drank like life depended on it, ate like life depended on it, laughed like life depended on it, argued like life depended on it.

Had relationships like life depended on them.

Had friendships like life depended on them.

But if all that follows reads like a love story, that's what it was.

—You can fuck off if you think you're eating that in this car, Dad said.

—You know scientists fed rats sauerkraut for a year? I said.

—Did the rats grow up to be as clever as you? he said. One day, I'm going to tell the story about the morning I drove you to the airport to go to London and you had a packed lunch that smelled like the bin.

One of these conversations was going to be our last for some time, we both knew it. The usual courtesies came to mind—staying in touch, making sure I had the address of his cousin's place in Crouch End, money to spare.

I pulled an old favourite from the repertoire. Every family had its own language, and we'd made ours through anagrams.

—Eric Clapton, he said.

—Narcoleptic, I said. My turn. Britney Spears.

—Presbyterian, he said.

—Villainousness.

—No idea, Dad said.

—An evil soul's sin. Conversation?

—You tell me, he said.

—Voices rant on.

—Too easy, he said. You make it look too easy.

We parked up and went into the terminal. There was time before I had to go through to departures. I had some of my food and there was this, that and the other from Dad about my first big summer away from home.

—I wish you'd lay off all that, I said.

—Whenever I bring it up, you go a bit incommunicado.

—Because I'm embarrassed, I said. You should try it.

But Dad got to hear all about university at the end of the summer: my new friends and where they might be from and all the different subjects they'd study and what good it was going to do them if they weren't going to be a doctor like me.

—Go on, he said. Put me out of my misery.

My boarding pass was out, and I joined the queue, this boy who loved games (cause games had rules), and who still saw the point of them.

Dad said, —Look behind you. See those security guards?

—I'm not doing anything wrong, I said.

—This might be the first time they've ever pulled someone in for having an explosive substance in their sandwich.

It wasn't that I didn't like the house; it just needed a haircut, all the ivy.

You were supposed to admire a place being this ramshackle. A riot of bric-a-brac, skid-marked chintz and all sorts of mad porcelain. The sloping floorboards, windows that wouldn't close, tiles so old that they looked dusty when they weren't.

Lovely for those who liked that kind of thing, and Tommy Carmody did seem to like that kind of thing.

Seventeen, just left school, free to go where I pleased. At night I'd squeeze myself into an alcove in the living room and wait for someone to walk in.

Things everywhere.

White shirts from someplace called Dries Van Noten; very dark and heavy Japanese Levis; smart suit after smart suit, and as many pairs of brogues as a person would have pairs of socks.

The clothes were scattered in the living room, and the hall, and piled on his bed, which was dressed like something from a hotel, and flanked by two shell-covered dressing tables whose drawers I was desperate to open.

Was there a need to justify the presence of those books in the bath, the surfboard in the kitchen? Why were there three very expensive acoustic guitars but no music system? Why was there a bronze bust of Lady Gregory but no mirror in the bathroom?

I know how corny it sounds, but this was a house with a restless heart.

The irregularities in the decor—three hat-racks but no toaster—had to be down to someone's absence. One room on the ground floor was completely empty but for floorboards ablaze with paint splashes of so many colours.

The house had its own smell, too.

A few old bottles of cologne in the bathroom, but this wasn't it. The smell seemed to come out of the walls or the woodwork. It wasn't in any way animal, but the mildness had something to do with the body; it had something to do with skin, sweet-smelling skin.

The bedroom at the very top of the stairs was all I had been hoping for. There was foliage brushing the window, and just enough sky. No stars at night but the morning light was enough to support me through those moments when I missed my mother (who was gone anyway) and my father (who'd needed me gone).

The house was saying: there's something I'd like to show you about life. When I listen, I am sure I can hear the words in Tommy's voice.

In the first few days of being his mystery lodger, or the lodger to a mystery, I thought about very little other than Tommy Carmody.

It's a puzzle I'm still figuring out. I worked through it on my walks to work, an hour there and back, past Highgate Cemetery and through Hampstead Heath, gathering my spirits for days on a building site peopled by nine IRA men and one Rastafarian (probably IRA, too).

The job was a gut renovation of a house the size of a small hospital.

The client was being slow in his paying his bills and the foreman, Noel, was reciprocating by stalling progress on the kitchen extension. In one day, I was passed from brick-stacking to bricklaying to roofing to landscape gardening; clearing the rubble and levelling the ground in readiness for its new layer of turf which Noel said might well be slow in arriving.

Even before I'd met him, I was planning to fill Tommy in on the best way to take a nap in the ripper of a bulldozer.

Any man who owned that many hammocks would understand.

One Friday I bought some chips on the way home to have with a can of cider in the garden; coming home to a message on the machine that Tommy might be in Morocco, or he might be in Toulon, or he might have moved on to Paris, in which case he might be back later, or the next day, or the day after that.

Soon, anyway, the message said.

Ciao, it said.

The garden wasn't even a garden, more a slope with a very old glasshouse and some terraces that had been cut and planted on and then abandoned. There was a big, hairy tree coming up through the patio.

The glasshouse didn't have much going for it, either.

Countryside smells in the middle of the city, armchairs you couldn't sit in. But if I played my cards right,

I supposed this could be mine while I left my landlord to his strange perambulations indoors.

After so long away, Tommy would want to make himself at home, at home.

I'd taken a copy of W.B. Yeats's letters to read with my dinner, but there was only so much dear-dainty-delicious-darling a young heart could take, and I was ready for a doze.

The voice that woke me said, —You'll have to play your filthy games elsewhere.

My copy of the letters was turned up on the page where the poet says, 'I kiss your hands' to his wife to be.

—Muck, he said. Sorry if you didn't hear me clearing my throat.

—You didn't, I said.

He held up my can of cider, sniffed its contents and made a show of not saying a word.

I'd seen him in pictures but Tommy Carmody, in person, managed to be both brutish and babyish. His hair was hanging long and loose like a fern. The clothes were for the heat and probably to dictate a mood.

You don't hurry anyone in a sarong.

—Don't you believe that I was reading? I said.

—Looking at you, yes, I do, he said.

There was a folding chair by the door of the glasshouse. The chair creaked as he sat into it.

—I know what you're thinking, he said.

—Do you? I said.

—You're always thinking something, he said.

He smelled expensively of thyme and wet cement.

I snapped up the book, the blood rising from my thighs to my cheeks. It wasn't a habit of mine to go anywhere without a goodbye or hello, but at least I closed the glass-house door after me.

At least he'd been shown that I hadn't been born in a barn.

Tommy took up the folding chair and came outside. He had the chair in two hands and seemed to change his mind just as he was about to throw it away up the garden.

—I bet your dad's chairs don't creak, he said.

—I dare say they don't.

His voice was straight from *My Fair Lady*. —You dare say?

In love with the fact that I had nearly made him laugh, I said, —I could get you a chair from inside.

—Dear boy, would you? Draw me a bath or what have you.

Barbecues a few doors down, the chitchat muffled by the breeze and all that sky. Nine at night and warm as it had been in the middle of the day.

Wasn't it this: wasn't it purple skies I'd come away from home for?

—And what will we say to the neighbours? Tommy said.

—Why would we want to say anything?

—They'll invite us over for a drink, he said.

—It doesn't sound like the kind of affair that requires invitations, I said.

He was getting ideas. Likely they were never that far away.

The cider got poured down the drain and out came a leather holdall containing six bottles of Champagne, and as many candlesticks. Never happy until any space he was in contained so much old wood and so many candles that there was the risk it of it burning down.

—Taking us all with it, he said, the tone of voice suggesting hooch and cigars and old-time beatings given as a warning.

He'd liberated the candlesticks from the props department on the movie.

He flopped down in the grass beside me to pour some more Champagne, spilling so much that he may as well have thrown it from across the garden.

—How were the musketeers? I said.

Tommy had the habit—I am sure it was practised—of seeming to think too much about every question. Was it an actor's way of prolonging the shot and drawing the scene towards them?

—Glorious, he said.

—I'm not sure I know what one is.

—I've just lost the waxed moustache. Start there. At least now I can shoot a crossbow. Endless ridiculousness.

Tommy Carmody was what you'd call a character actor; his face was the special effects.

The director of the musketeers film, known for making

commercials with flying elephants in them, preferred looking at his storyboards to what was happening right there in front of him, and Tommy preferred films where people walked around and said things to each other.

The neighbours were still warming up and Tommy went to the fence to cock an ear. Someone was playing 'Eternal Flame', and he began to sing along.

—Music that's been soaked in butter, he said.

Then he let out a sudden roar of, —She is a lovely, lovely woman!

The words hung so long in the air—like the neighbours' washing—that I wanted to take them down and put them away.

If it was all I was getting on the end of Tommy's marriage, he let me know that it would be perfectly normal to see him drinking in the mornings, and that he almost never sat down to breakfast or lunch when you were supposed to. Bedtime was often half four in the afternoon.

There was something deeply sad to this man about doing things at the right times. He knew of these things and believed in them in the same way that people thought of the Loch Ness monster.

And his idea of exercise was to check into a hotel to order room service and watch sport on satellite TV.

He wasn't any kind of role model at all.

It was past midnight when he decided on a barbecue of our own. I helped him drag the wood and everything from the glasshouse and soon we were talking over each other about meals we'd eaten outdoors and all the times we'd slept under the stars (I was having to make things up).

There was a moon around somewhere, and it wasn't so dark that we couldn't see that the plants were drowsy from the heat.

Tommy unrolled the hose and watered everything while I fussed about with courgettes and aubergines that he'd brought back from France and dug around for herbs—there was mint and whatnot growing in pots—and then we sat with nothing to do but drink and drink without feeling drunk.

—What do you think of the garden? he said.

—Pretty full on, I said. The colours.

—I'd like to say I've planned it, but it just does its own thing when I'm away. Plenty of green, plenty of red. Goes easy on the yellow.

—Wise, I said. You might need to get some gardening things.

—And someone to do the gardening, Tommy said.

It was going to take the fire a long time to burn down the way he wanted it to. He wanted us to cook on the embers like they did in Morocco (he'd done some films there).

Working in the way that Tommy did, travelling the world to be in things, seemed like a total fantasy and the most sensible thing in the world.

Now he was talking about how he had gone about

finding this house in much the same way as he'd sign onto a film; he'd wanted to work in France so much that he hadn't bothered reading the script for the film he'd just been in.

He was talking about moving there. But it's not a holiday if you live someplace, he said.

I had a strong urge to say Tommy behaved like he was a visitor in his own house. Clothes in the hall. Everything else somewhere else.

Once I'd known him for longer, I'd be able to say it.

We'd be the kind of friends who could share such things.

He decided the fire was ready to add the vegetables. And he said, —What do you like to do, Ian? When you're not having fun.

That took some thought.

The end of school had held no more surprises than the psychometric stuff they put you through in the final year. I had some questions of the methodology, and I had had to laugh at the result—Ian Cleary is data driven, Ian Cleary is cold.

My teachers didn't want to hear that the experiment was flawed and gave me top marks anyway.

But I'd just had my big science brain to thank for a trip to Paris.

I would win every competition in my path and come up with ludicrous new challenges for myself: behavioural sciences or neuroscience, I couldn't decide. Things We Say in Our Dreams. It was my least favourite of all the ideas, but it meant Paris: dreams meant winning a trip Paris, yes.

Dad bought me every new thing and stuffed me with enough cash for a blowout in a casino. Meanwhile there were other people, and they had won prizes, too, and if they weren't as smart as I was, they were very smart, and they were so happy to be there that I felt ashamed of being so shy, and there were other things too: I felt the age gap so badly that even though I could try the science stuff I couldn't do the chit-chat at all.

The conference organiser said she liked the shirt Dad had bought me; the woman in the hotel gave me a chocolate mint, and Dad bought a ticket and got on a plane to take me home. He asked if I'd seen the note on my luggage—how proud he was, how clever he thought I was—but I hadn't unpacked enough to find it. I hadn't worn half the nice shirts I'd been bought, and I hadn't thought of it once until now.

—That's a big one, Tommy said.

—Bit much?

—Not at all, he said. Not at all.

—There are some games I like to play, I said.

Anagrams were one thing. And even though I wasn't the best in the world at them, tongue twisters were a form of meditation. I tripped up all the time, sometimes I couldn't get through a classic like Betty bought a bit of butter.

Your throat got tangled up, or your mouth dried up like you'd eaten too many crackers. But when I was on form, when that happened, I would sit in the school library and instead of studying I'd make my way through the most difficult one of all.

Pad kid poured curd pulled cod.

Tommy went to the glasshouse to get a pair of torches, and I shone mine at the ground. The light reflecting from the grass made it look like he had been painted in water-colours. He wasn't there in front of me, he was a picture hanging on a wall, one you could study.

His face looked very lightly on fire.

Was there a knack to tongue twisters, he wanted to know. What was the trick? Breathing? Throat? Brain?

I said there were front-of-the-tongue sounds, sea-shells and seashores, back-of-the-tongue sounds, and lip sounds, and yes, the brain got busy with it all.

You just had to take your time. Go as slowly as a pen-sioner, and even then, you were never completely sure of yourself, especially when there were other things on your mind.

And Tommy was right, and I did think hard about things.

Mum once said that if you went through life with love, you not only increased the aggregate amount of it in the world, as made perfect sense, you saw some of it back.

Interest on your deposits.

And saving was never a bad idea.

Neither a morning nor an evening person, I had never been at this side of a dawn.

Coming down the hill into Crouch End, being so careful to notice everything. A single column of cloud in the sky, the pointed shadows of the church. Someone's washing was soaked on a line. The rooftops and houses looking so clean from the rain, pavements glittering as they dried.

The village would never be as beautiful as this.

I was going to bring something home for Tommy's breakfast, and I was trying to ignore the fact that he had disappeared to bed without saying goodbye.

We had larked about for hours, only thinking to leave when the storm came in and soaked the fire.

There were one or two moments, with birdsong competing with night sounds, that I felt myself being scrutinised. The combination of amusement and dissatisfaction that Tommy Carmody specialised in.

The performer judging his audience.

Whenever I'd thought it was time to go to bed, Tommy appeared with something else to put on the fire—onions, peppers brought back from France.

I took whatever he bundled into my arms before licking it with oil and setting it into the fire where it would be cajoled into mouthfuls that made me want do something I had never done before, which was to record all this in a journal (the one I've been keeping all these years); not just the food, but the embers, and the trees in the darkness.

Tommy, most of all.

This was why, hardly an hour or two later, it felt like

all of this had happened last week or last year, and I was replaying every single moment, turning each one over in the hope that it may contain a trace of a trace of something that I could carry and keep as I drifted off to sleep later.

Tommy had been paying close attention to a fire that seemed to be looking after itself. Onions baking on an old roof tile, other things blackening in the embers. I could smell garlic but couldn't see it. Perhaps it was buried.

He'd taken an onion from the fire and bitten into it. (And like much of what attaches itself to Tommy, I don't know if it ever happened.)

His face started to move and then settled.

He waited, and then I did. As soon as a thought would form it could not make itself into the kind of words that I could say to someone like Tommy Carmody.

Or I'd find the right words, but not the moment.

Perhaps I was experiencing what many people of that age succumb to: nostalgia for the moment you've never known. The feeling is called anemoia but it's more bearable when you don't know the word.

And was it then, when he ate the entire onion, that I knew we'd be friends for life?

If you're lucky, all you need is one of those.

I was on my way up to my room in the attic when I saw that his door was open. Tommy lying on the floor beside the bed.

This was, I supposed, something he was doing on purpose.

It was not how I'd expected the night to end, completely silent on his part, terrified on mine. I waited for him to say something, so I could say something, and the night could wind down in a shared moment.

I listened for a breath. There might have been a sigh.

I said, —Are you all right?

—Yes, he said, quietly.

On the floor beside him were more snapshots—a hat he'd been wearing on the film, another sarong he'd brought out to lay over the hay bales. Except for a wrung-out Turkish towel, the mattress was completely bare.

—What are you doing down there?

—Trying to sleep, he said.

—Do you need anything? I said.

—Can you please close the door? he said.

—Sure, I said.

—I'd like to be alone, he said.

—Sure.

—In a please be somewhere else kind of way.

I had long since let go of any memory of my mother. Ten years since she had prayed her way into peace in life and onwards towards the next one.

To die on a Sunday was part of an ongoing conversation with You Know Who, or a demonstration of her faith that I was too young to share, and that she was happy to have to herself.

Anything else that remained of my childhood was the knowledge that something had always been the matter with her.

We had been on a family holiday in north Clare, and she had gone out walking alone. She had been walking for ages without noticing anyone behind her on the beach. When she did notice me, she didn't talk for most of the day, except to ask me why I had followed her.

Mum explained that she was glad of her own company from time to time, and next time that happened, she'd turn me around for home. Later, when she called me in for supper, she fell into more of an explanation of why she liked to go out walking on her own.

She was making pancakes, piling them up and counting them out.

Mum brought the pancakes to the table on separate plates for everyone. It's just like eating off your own plate, she said. Sometimes, being a mummy was like getting to the table for dinner only to find everyone helping themselves to your food, especially when they have plenty of their own to eat.

By the time I got some sleep, Tommy had been out for bread but came back with two kilos of langoustines.

One little place had the only bread he'd wanted but the baker was indisposed and even though Tommy would have been better off going somewhere else, perhaps for what he'd gone out for, he decided to mark the occasion of having a new lodger.

—So what's for lunch? he said.

—You tell me, I said.

—Prawns are what's for lunch.

He was now in such a good mood that he may as well have gone about the place in clown's shoes, honking his red nose.

We built another fire, and the prawns got cooked in something like a cauldron and he served them in a bucket which we ate from, sitting on those hay bales.

The first prawn was gone in one-two-three.

The next one, he coached me on how to pierce the flesh to remove the shit-sack.

—You're a pro, Tommy said.

—I'm sure we can't have prawns every day, I said.

—We can, he said.

He decided against more to drink, but if he said so himself, Tommy Carmody was famous for his lunches. His dinners involved people taking annual leave from work. Sometimes the serving of actual food came as a shock to people.

He had some more ideas; with this knack for looking desolate but sounding cheerful—which I may have had, too, but the other way around.

The point was, if this was to be my first big summer, he'd take on the job personally.

It was no accident that he'd chosen to live in a

neighbourhood without a tube. If I was up for getting around the place, Tommy would walk me through London. This was a city for seeing on foot.

If there was good stuff to do, we'd do it, galleries and gigs and things but most of the best messing—and messing was a form of exaltation—happened in parks.

Frisbees, bottles of cava drunk from paper cups, girls, girls with frisbees and drinking cava from paper cups.

We shook on it.

The excitement of a city with so many colours.

The excitement of a girl who might be interested in you, the ones who aren't, the excitement of songs blasting from speeding taxis, from open windows, the excitement of an empty park at dawn, and busy at twilight, honey skies, vivid heat, the excitement of nightfall, the excitement of not being home and home being nowhere from now on.

—We'll have a right old time of it, Tommy said.

We were finished eating and I took a newspaper and wrapped the prawn shells in it, carrying them away as carefully as someone removing a child from a bath.

One day in Tommy's company had made me want to do everything right. But my brain was tired, it had been studying day and night. The cognitive process experienced by a clinician in a triage ward was not the same as for a GP and was not the same as for a surgeon.

I would have to figure that out.

In the meantime, there was a weekend to be savoured.

Tommy said there wouldn't be another one like it, and

everywhere I looked there was a box or a drawer from which he would produce a jar of olives from two trips ago; or a notebook from a hotel in Montreal that he'd use for sketching out routes from Crouch End to wherever we could walk to in half a day.

Tommy went inside to get a map.

It was a very good thing, in my opinion, to work from a plan.

One of his ideas—long stored up, I think—was for us to get up first thing in the morning and walk two, three or four hours to somewhere like Brixton.

This would be another London altogether. I could make it my own.

And when I went to get a tray to clear up the plates, Tommy told me why he'd been lying on the floor of his room the night before.

He couldn't sleep in a bed cause *she* used to sleep in that bed.

And it hurt too much to sleep in a bed *she* had once slept in.

Tommy still wasn't telling me who *she* was, but love was becoming our specialised subject. He would talk about it incessantly and in the abstract.

Love was You Know What.

The people who cared most about You Know What were the ones who'd known the most unhappiness cause of it.

It was either voluntary or involuntary, not that anyone knew the difference at the time. Was love something you did or did love happen to you? Love happens, Tommy said. It's a happening thing.

And afterwards?

You can't be your own complaints department, he said.

The way Tommy put it, falling in love was as essential and as everyday as going out for bread but buying prawns.

Since Mum died, anyone new who crossed my path, I tried to love them with all my heart. Friends, strangers, people on the bus, the priests at school, Dad, the list went on.

Never mind making lists: love made love, and confusion made more confusion. Every girl I'd ever met was an alien or a mannequin.

The best I could ever hope was to appear distracted—and absent-minded, deaf, dumb and blind—in female company, and to have it that I was taken by surprise by them.

They were a them.

We'd gone to schools a few minutes' walk from each other, and even though she lived in Clontarf, and I lived in Glenageary, I used to wait with Rosemary Walton for her Dart every day after school.

Sometimes I got on the train and walked her all the way up from the station to her house, before taking the train all the way home.

We did this for weeks, then months.

Winter appeared and the streetlights came on, seeming to pose the question of when we were going to get on with it.

It being You Know What.

We agreed very quickly that things wouldn't go any further than holding hands until the exams were out of the way. I sailed through mine, and the day we finished, Rosemary surprised me with the kissing of my life; and tickets to see *Cinema Paradiso* at the Screen.

The film was one of her favourites and she wanted us to watch it together.

I fell asleep for a little while at the start—it had been a long few weeks—and when I woke up, I couldn't follow what was going on. But Rosemary had finally let go of my hand and I thought about all the magnificent piazze and the benevolence of the buildings in the film and how it would be easy to fall in love there, somewhere very far away from where I was from.

That Saturday continued at a pace I would grow used to.

Once we'd finished lunch, I can admit to being a little relieved when Tommy went inside to unpack. This involved walking from room to room, a stranger in his own house, stopping to look at the back of a picture or pick up a seashell like it was unfamiliar to him, like he was wondering whether to keep it or throw it away.

He must have known that I'd be taking all of this in.

And there was the small matter of running a bath and

letting it sit while I went to my room to get a towel and finding Tommy up to his chin in the water.

—That's mine, I said.

—It's my house, he said.

—But I ran the bath.

—It just looked so nice, Tommy said.

The trick was to make out you were taking everything in your stride.

I could hear him playing guitar in the bath, and when the evening came the sun softened enough for him to come out to the garden. Very little of the moment shows up for me now, as I go looking to recall it, but I was overwhelmed in Tommy's company and perhaps embarrassed, for reasons I still can't name.

Me, the garden bench, the glasshouse, the firepit, the hay bales, the ferns and trees, we were being sung to, and I was going to be about as animated and responsive as they were.

The sound of his playing was sweet as something you'd hear in a dream, and I wondered if this was down to his soft playing style or the tuning of the instrument. Mostly it was the guitar but once or twice he began singing, repeating a line as though he was writing something or trying to learn a song.

He'd make sure to catch my eye to make sure that I'd got it, too; the big melody and the mood joining as instructions to memorise the words.

A dream much too real to be leaned against too long.

The thoughts did not come to me so neatly at the time,

but the sound of an unaccompanied voice can make anyone feel very lonely. But that summer London was not a lonely place.

If life was sweet, what else was sweet?

The night sky from my bedroom was minty sweet.

Crouch Hill was a sweet incline, the air up here sweeter than the air down there in the city.

Two hundred and eighty pounds a week into my paw at the end of a week, double time for a Saturday, sweet as a nut.

I could pay for taxis, I could pay for pizza, and wine.

I could pay for a new pair of Levi's every week, if I wanted to, which was a reminder that I had never bought my own clothes before, which was a reminder that my mother would have told me I looked silly in that paisley bandana.

Wine was sweet, only if it was Lambrusco, which was also the wrong wine, and which Tommy wouldn't allow over the threshold, and which he'd get me to drink on the doorstep or return it to the shop.

The juice he'd squeezed for me in the morning was fruity sweet.

Bittersweetness was sweet.

I was being introduced to the wonder and dirt and difficulty of a new city, the cleverness of a vast and new city, the cleverness of Tommy, of course, and my cleverness, newly discovered, in a city and a summer that wouldn't end.

London smelled excitingly of sewers and sweat, mown lawns, and very pronouncedly of dope-smoke, a combination I did not try to make sense of. But as I got the hang of life on a building site (keep moving, always carry something, always best to be smoking something), there was no other purpose in life but to be where Tommy was, no other purpose than to absorb and imitate his way of pursuing the business of pleasure.

Now and then I would call in sick or ask to be let off early, and even if my job and my future had been on the line, it wouldn't have mattered cause I was meeting Tommy to go to a play at the National, then for a steak in Covent Garden.

Steaks at ten o'clock at night!

I had never eaten pasta cooked by anyone I wasn't related to, and soon I found myself eating fettuccine with people who'd been in Mike Leigh films.

Sometimes Tommy seemed to be enjoying himself at these dinners, sometimes he didn't. I couldn't work it out, but when something seemed to be bothering him, he/we sought the soothing effects of love.

The sight of someone passingly attractive, in a cafe or a car, would make him momentarily reflective before his heart would bubble over with the bewitching sight of someone putting their hair up in a bun, their hair coming down, their hair on the pillow or on his chest.

Then he'd go quiet again, and we'd cover more of London, all with sense that we would never be done with the subject.

If I never knew where we were going on our walks, Tommy and I would usually end up in Soho (usually the Coach & Horses; acting seemed to be a profession in which it was socially acceptable to be an alcoholic), and often we would take a detour through Savile Row to get there.

Every now and again, after a big job, Tommy would reward himself with a bespoke suit (the ones that hung likes spectres in his wardrobe), and he was quite convinced I needed one too. I'd be learning all about anatomy in medical school, and it turned out there were just as many ways of cutting a suit as there were types of body.

And a visit to a tailor's shop wasn't the worst way of spending an hour or two.

If an object passed through his hands to mine—a spare white shirt, a pen with just the right clip to sit in the pocket of that shirt—it assumed a kind of all-time magic.

He was always on the phone. He'd go to his room or out to the garden to take the calls.

He claimed not to know anyone, but he seemed to know everyone.

In these calls, he took on so many personae, all of them new to me and ill-fitting on him, as if he was a salesman peddling only the versions of himself that might impress the art people, the film people, the fashion people that he liked to talk to.

I mastered the art of partaking in the conversations without saying a word.

I'd also found some new French folk music to catch his attention, and like he was phoning for a pizza, Tommy arranged for us to go to the band's gig in Kentish Town.

These things—phone calls, guest-lists—seemed to take no effort.

I sense an evening out is in order, he'd say. On me.

It's always on you, I'd say.

Tommy said to take a half-day from the site, and first to meet him in Soho. I came straight from work, mud stains all the way down the thighs of my jeans. Brick dust in my hair.

—Very rock & roll, he said. Insouciant.

I think I enjoyed that he'd cared enough to say something.

We got to Andrew Edmunds just in time for last orders at lunch. The table he headed straight towards was about the size of a coat pocket but had a nice view of the street.

The exuberance of all the lunches just winding up around us.

He was not very famous, but Tommy Carmody's was a vaguely well-known face. The posh hair, the boyish plumpness in the chin and, as they were leaving the restaurant, many people said hello to him, some so cheerfully that he wondered if he had paid their bill.

He spied some old Rioja and some young Beaujolais, and the prospect of wine made everything else seem a bit more interesting and optimistic. There was a point halfway down the second bottle of something where we went through some kind of secret door.

The food was coming and going, and wine was coming and going, and people, too, and Tommy's attitude to life began to soften.

What were we going to do when all of this was over? he wondered.

Afterwards, the pavements were stirring, streets alive, taxis blithely idling. We took one to Kentish Town.

It was another sugary, hot evening and we were sculling pints on the pavement next to the venue when there was a kerfuffle and we were jostled by a bunch of guys looking like down-on-their-luck gangsters in a film noir.

Tall, skinny, grey suits, hats with rims.

A few curses in French, and I half-recognised the tiny man in a string vest and high-waisted pleated trousers. In hands the size of a child's, he was carrying three large bloody marys, drinking from each one in turn.

This was the band we'd come to see, and this was their singer, Mlah. The febrile demeanour was heightened by the recognition around us.

Someone called out that they should do the gig right here, and the bloody marys got handed off—one got downed—and the little guy began dancing.

Mlah was moving like a very earnest and uncoordinated puppet, twitching, hair plastered to his head with sweat and whatever else. When his band mates saw what he was up to, they moved either side of him to stand guard.

He began on a medley of, I don't know, verses, lines and improvisations.

The more animated Mlah was, the more impassive they were.

Expressions empty, gazes endless.

They were like sentries until, as one, their arms went out, horizontally, palms rotating.

—Hup! they were shouting. Hup!

Something else was happening, too. Mlah was slowly wetting himself.

The patch bloomed slowly, darkening in an almost melodic way. It was noticed by one of the sentries, who didn't belabour the fact of wrapping his coat around the singer's waist.

Mlah, who wanted to finish the song, didn't seem to notice. As they were taking him away, he was drinking the last of a bloody mary.

One of the luckiest and best things about becoming Tommy's friend—the greatest privilege of them all—was that I was beginning to feel what he was feeling.

And I was accustomed to him suddenly departing the moment whenever it wasn't meeting with his approval.

He was looking at the door of the bar for a long time before he told me that he'd seen his ex-wife go inside.

I heard him say, —She looked so nice.

—It was going to happen sooner or later, he said.

They hadn't spoken since she'd left.

She had moved into a place in Camden while they were figuring out what to do with the divorce. He'd offered her the house in Crouch End, but she had her own money and didn't want any of his.

I'd never seen anyone look so exhausted, and there wasn't much likelihood of going to the gig. We'd already seen more than enough of Mlah.

Tommy walked up to the door of the bar, pausing there a moment.

The breeze was lifting his hair; his eyes were shut. Slowly he turned and began to walk away, but with an absolute sense of purpose.

Nothing Tommy ever did seemed to lack intent, but I felt his hopelessness. So it is when you watch someone being left to their fate.

Rosemary Walton asked me to her Debs. Once Dad had dropped me off to her house, I ran back to the car to ask a question.

All our friends wanted to drink, but we didn't want to. Was that okay? It was okay, Dad said.

Around midnight, our agreed time, Dad found me sitting on the front steps of the hotel. It wasn't what I'd meant to happen, I said, and it wasn't what Rosemary had expected, and it wasn't the night for it to take place.

I don't think Dad knew which part of this evaluation he was supposed to consider first.

We had agreed we wouldn't drink; no one was that bothered with it anyway. But someone had cider, and some vodka appeared, different kinds of fruity stuff, that was the problem, the fruity booze was so tasty and once everyone else was going to, Rosemary didn't see any harm in having one or two. And I shouldn't have said what I said.

Some awful words passed between us.

There was no way of knowing if Rosemary got more upset cause she was so drunk. She accused me of being mean; cause I'd been mean. I'd told her I'd have preferred to have come alone, and the sharpness of my own words had caught me off guard.

Love ought not to have been so difficult.

Now Rosemary walked across the car park with her friends.

Someone had her shoes; she had someone else's coat on.

It looked as though I was the only one going home in the clothes I had gone out in.

I took my father's advice to stay put but was almost shaking as I got into the car. I didn't need his help with the seatbelt, but I was checking the mirrors were still in place. Don't mind that, Dad said, as if all the things I did out of good conscience were for my own benefit.

I waved to Rosemary's friends, and Dad took my hand.

His son, so obstinate and sad.

Then one of them—the girl with Rosemary's shoes

in her hands—appeared at our windscreen to land a big chunk of fruity phlegm on it.

—Shall we head for home? Dad said.

—We could have stayed there, I said.

—No, you had to come out. Big nights, things happen.

—Big night, I said.

I waited a few moments before getting out of the car and wiping the glass with my sleeve.

The man walking alone up Kentish High Road was an expert on You Know What.

He was the expert on mellifluous silences.

He was the expert on stony silences.

He was the expert on loving love, on praising it to the high heavens.

He was the expert in being out of love.

By the time I had caught up with him, halfway to Archway, Tommy was deep in conversation with himself, the words sounding as if they had been scripted and the lines were being delivered by a good actor.

Such a good actor that each phrase sounded like it was it just occurring to him. The actor in him reminding me that life was a play, and sometimes it was an absurd and sad one.

Before I followed him home, I'd looked into the bar but hadn't seen anyone who looked they might have been Tommy's ex-wife. One of the reasons why I'd never recognised anyone who might have resembled a wife of

Tommy Carmody was that she was fifty-five years old. He was thirty.

Niamh Ahern.

Painter.

Ahead of her time.

Tommy described this woman with great reverence.

It wasn't just that Niamh Ahern, the fifty-five-year-old painter, had run away with his heart. He was in love with the way she was in love with her work. He loved her when she was asleep, he loved her in the morning, he'd love her when she was older still.

What was the job of a marriage but to weave all this together?

But somewhere along the way, they had lost the ability to communicate.

Tommy liked to work.

If he was in a play, life was the play.

The rest of the time he was either away, or preparing to be, and he spent so much time away from home that when he'd come back, it felt like he was visiting Niamh in her studio. When Tommy thought of his ex-wife, he pictured her in action, in overalls; the soft, careful gestures she'd make around a work-in-progress; the care she'd take over preparing to work, and the work itself.

And you can't leave someone to do their own thing and then be upset that they do exactly that.

—I'm driving myself loolah, he said. When a marriage is a going concern, you don't question it. If you did, you might see how fucking flimsy the whole thing is.

Terror blazed quickly across his face. Then, likely in an effort to disappear themselves, his features folded over one another. Not an image I can easily confront, and not one I've ever been able to absorb, Tommy Carmody crying.

Heartbreak. You can fall in love with heartbreak, and I was falling in love with his.

He said, —There's nothing like a summer's night for making you feel you've made an awful bollix of things. It's like a lullaby being sung for someone else. Where's my fucking lullaby? Not exactly rational, not entirely adult. We'd talk, anyway. Any amount of calls, any amount of talking, we'd be on the phone until the sun came up, but we couldn't contact each other. Which I noticed at the time, I even said so. If we're away from each other let's be away, but when we're home let's be home? But Niamh wanted to talk more. So, it was put to me, let's get away on a trip.

I was going to be a doctor one day and everything Tommy had been saying to me about love had behind it a diagnosis he didn't want to acknowledge.

His heart was desolated; it was empty.

—The plan was a little Seville, he said. A little Jerez, and then we'd end up by the sea in Sanlúcar de Barrameda. We used to go there for the bullfighting, and sherry. Thirty or forty very small beers and it feels like you haven't been drinking. So we bounced off the plane, bad knee and all, but we'd nothing booked. Then Niamh decided that she wanted to be by the sea straightaway. I could have done with a little saltwater myself. But there in the queue for the hire car, she was getting at the fact that I like to control things, which was also fair enough, but cause we hadn't booked anything, there was only a small Seat. Or a minibus. Now, this was a very small car, and this was going to be a pow-wow kind of thing. Do you want to be having one of those in a very small space? So, we opted for the minibus; it was a brute, the pair of us said it at the same time. You could smell something; I'm sure it was carcasses, but I kept that to myself. My leg wasn't great, and Niamh said she'd drive, and by the time we'd got to Sanlúcar we were dying from the heat, but we got a nice room in a nice place. Sea breeze, thanking you. We tried making love, agreed to come back to it, but the intent was there, and we sat on the balcony for a few glasses, a salted almond, a bit of ham, very nice ham altogether, and she said she was going out to check on the minibus. Strange enough. It had got us there in one piece, I thought we'd leave it to its own devices in the garage for a while. And when she got back to the room, she took all the spare blankets they have stowed away, and a pillow, and she made a bed for the night in the back of the smelly bus. I needed to be in a proper bed, but I said we could get two rooms, if she wanted her own space. There was no need to spend that night in a fucking HiAce smelling of sheep. And she gave it a bit of thought. We were due to be there for a week, it would be uncomfortable, she agreed. I reckoned I could persuade her to at least get a room in another hotel, she could be there, getting a proper night's rest.

As we came up the hill into Crouch End, Tommy began looking over hedges. Standing at gates.

Every house looked like it was preferable to him to the one he was going back to.

—It used to get to her that I've never been good at sleeping through the night. We'd make love and I'd stay there until she had fallen asleep and I'd either go downstairs or next door. She'd ask me why I had to go, then she told me that it felt like I'd sleep in any room in the house except the one she was in. There was always a reason to be somewhere else. Bad knee, sore back, snoring, the flu, I tried to tell her that all I'd be doing was keeping her awake. If Niamh needed me in the night, all she had to do was come and get me. Or she could call out and I'd answer, or I'd come in to her if I was up, which I usually was. I'm not a child, she said, don't try and treat me like one. That wasn't what I meant at all. I made her lonely in her own life.

Loneliness worried me more than anyone else. I'd never thought of it as something another person could cause.

—Did she sleep in the bus? I asked.

—All week. It was parked up in the same place in the garage; I thought she might take off, but she spent every night in it. I don't know what she did in the day. We landed back in London without saying another word. And when we got home, she told me why she'd gone to sleep there. She always felt I had her where I wanted her. Up on a shelf. In a little glass case. Admire but don't touch. That's when Niamh decided to go somewhere where I would never go looking. She wanted somewhere that was just for her. I would have picked a few places better than that bus, and I still can't get over the smell of fucking pig. But that's the picture she wanted me to keep. Minibus, blankets. Then she looked at me with the saddest eyes and told me she didn't want to be married any more.

When we got home, Tommy and I stood in the garden.

The old tree was coming up through the patio. While it had to be older than the house, Tommy thought the posture was good, the poise of an athlete in their reflective years. But it was doing goodness knows what to the foundations and he was in two minds on whether it should stay or go.

—What do you think to clearing a bit of the garden? he said.

—We could dig some beds, I said.

—There's plenty of room for more vegetables in our lives.

If we were talking ourselves onto a different track, I laughed till I was sore when Tommy imitated a talking mushroom.

Together we began on a backstory for the tree, going back to the time of the farms and little else, no village to speak of. Squirrels? Squirrels, fine, Tommy said. But a family of bats had hatched inside the trunk, and there were squirrels, too, of course, and beetles and worms and mites. Moss ran rampant.

Rampant!

He didn't want to go inside, did he?

He was as exhausted as I'd ever seen him (and this was a man who slept in half-hour bursts).

Tommy said he was only tired cause London was a tiring place. The joy of big cities—and the world had only four or five true cities—was that they would kick your ass from time to time.

None of which deterred him from suggesting a late bit of supper.

This involved the slow business of lighting a fire and waiting for it to get to where Tommy wanted it to. The other part of the plan involved asking me to open every bottle of wine in the fridge. I poured so many glasses that he asked for but hardly touched, but in terms of perfect scenarios, this was near enough it.

At that stage in my life, I was able to make a salad just by waving my hands at some vegetables.

The miracle of this garden at summer's end. Every time we sat out in it, I thought I might move closer to the magnetic core of a life that, for me, had hardly begun, and had been only half-occupied.

We baked some cheese in the fire, and Tommy spilled some honey that he didn't clear up and there were ants coming from all around to run up our legs.

But the garden could have been overrun by those insects, and what could you do but let it happen?

The lights were off inside, and the house was grey but at even this time of night, the sky was blue, pale and sparkling, and was almost too much for anything to be said about it; except, to me, it was saying: this is who you are now.

Who you are now is not real, it is better than that.

Life is not real; it is better than that.

One of the wines we were drinking came from some rough hilltop in France. No water, Tommy said, and the most brutal winds. If the vines need to struggle, they need to struggle, it's for the best. The land knows what to do and we don't need to do anything to help it.

He was licking his knife, fingers covered in ants.

And he was saying, —I feel like getting carried away. It's not the wine. Or it is the wine, but it's not that it's doing anything more than it ever does. But there's an energy in it; it's moving through me. Can you feel it?

I didn't have to answer. I reached for one of the glasses.

Mouthful after mouthful after mouthful.

—This feeling will last for ever, he said. When wine like this is in the glass and it is on song, and you are on song, it is the thing that makes life worth living.

Agitation behind the ribs, check.

Not really eating, check.

Not really sleeping, check.

Tommy was still up when I came down for work in the morning.

He'd been drinking wine and whiskey, and he asked if I wanted any breakfast. I don't think I'd ever seen him eat any. He was wearing a watch, which he never did, and his eyes kept travelling to the door.

The thing about being quiet and gentle is that people don't tend to notice you, they forget you're there. But Tommy looked so frightened that even my presence there, eating breakfast, was a threat to his safety.

This sparkling, sharp, clever man, the sadness slopping out of him like the scrambled eggs he made me.

I wanted to leave him alone and he wanted to be left alone but I couldn't go to work. Easier to be there and to look away, so as to feel it, too.

Not to share Tommy's sadness but have it as my own.

When I asked him what had happened after Niamh left, it turned out he'd only been clearing his throat the night before.

—The morning after we came back from Spain, Niamh told me she'd come back to the wrong house. She didn't spend another night here. I slept downstairs for the first few nights. In the mornings, I'd go and look in our room in case she'd come back in the night. Remember what I do for a living, I can occupy any headspace, so the rest of the time I just told myself she hadn't gone anywhere, she was just in the other room. But I didn't like to fall asleep cause I didn't like to wake up and be reminded that she wasn't next door. I was lucky that I could work, and I was lucky that the first film I signed on to came with a few weeks in the sun. The day before I left for set, I was messing about upstairs, talking to myself in the mirror in the spare room, doing my homework, studying my delivery, when someone passed me in the landing. I saw them pass in the mirror. I heard the door close in the bedroom. I waited another minute before going out to the landing. Someone was moving around. I called out and she answered. Is that you, darling? Yes, she said. What do you want? Oh, nothing, just checking you're there. I'm going downstairs, do you want anything? No, she said, but maybe we'll have dinner later. Catch up with ourselves. I hope you've made something nice. Sounds good, I said. And later, she came downstairs, and I had made something nice, and we had dinner as we always did.

Playing along was all I could do. It was the role I'd been assigned.

—Is Niamh here *now*? I said.

—Yes, Tommy said quickly. But his eyes were so far away when he said this.

—Where is she? I said.

—She's upstairs, asleep. Like, she was in that bar last night, in Kentish Town with her friends. Or maybe she went into the gig to see the fella who pissed his pants? As we were walking home, as far as I was concerned, Niamh was still at home. Just about to finish up a big painting, not quite done, there's a few days' work left in it. Now she's just about to hop in the shower. I'll have made something to eat, so she knows there is something if she wants it, but she doesn't take that many breaks, and the food will be there waiting for us. So, I'll heat that up and we'll have it later.

—That sounds like a good arrangement, I said.

—Love goes, Ian. If you don't look after it, it goes. Or you might be the most attentive fucker on the planet, and it might still go. I'm off, it says.

He was going to go away for a while, he said, but I was fine to stay in the house as long as I wanted.

And I wasn't to worry.

He'd be in touch.

It's normal to become attached to friends, it's normal to miss them when they go. Even when they're there, sometimes you fall behind, or they forget about you for a while, but you catch up with them or they come back for you.

I don't know why I had been so upset to see Tommy go.

Either it was cause I was sad for him, that he felt he had to go, and sad for myself cause there were so many things I had to become good at without him.

One day, in the glasshouse, as I was looking for shears to tackle the ivy by my bedroom window, I found a sheaf of articles clipped from magazines and newspapers from long enough ago for the paper to have curled and yellowed. The pictures were of Tommy as a young actor alongside Maggie Smith and Jeremy Irons.

The film was some period thing called *The Golden Rooftops*.

I'd never seen him look like that, so sweet, so girlish almost, luscious lips undermined by chubby cheeks, and none of the pugnaciousness of later years.

Is it in your thirties that sweetness falls away?

What does it get replaced by?

I took to watching his films, alone obviously, in the dark, and in the chair with one of his Savile Row suit jackets hanging on the back.

I didn't dare put it on.

I was so used to seeing Tommy falling out of a pub with a hatchet in the head (always in the first five minutes of a film) that I was very taken by the wording on the box for *The Golden Rooftops.* This one was praised for its delicacy and longing and many other adjectives to bring a colour to my cheeks.

His character was the private tutor for Maggie Smith's granddaughter. As the girl was not doing so well at her history of art, tutor, student, family and all decamped to Venice to scrutinise the Tintorettos up close.

There was something sparse, or reserved, about the art direction—barely any gondolier, no wide shots of sitting rooms—and in the writing, and in the acting, too; as if everyone had only met each other that morning.

But this was nothing I was used to watching; the scene where the granddaughter becomes frustrated at her vocabulary for brushwork and Tommy's guy takes her hand to lead her outside for a breather.

Watching it and watching it, often twice or three times in one go, imagining myself into the frame, with Tommy or instead of him, I certainly didn't want to think of it as romantic. Try as I might to dismiss it as corny, stale, clichéd, my involvement with this scene—the moment where they stood in silhouette by some shining water, and Tommy took her hand—was more lyrical than anything I had encountered in real life.

The film was like a song to me.

Even going along the street to work, I could play it out, hearing Tommy's odd English accent, replying to him in mine, every utterance rehearsed and replayed as if under the most fastidious direction. Most scenes had enough of Tommy in them to keep me interested. Carrying furniture up a tight staircase, sweeping out his attic bedroom, tidying a library as if his life depended on it.

Occasionally a gesture, caught in the freeze frame, revealed something new. The little revelations in a face, the blur between a smile and a frown, now as permanent and undeniable as a painting.

The pictures were asking me something: if I had gone beyond fascination, how far beyond it was I?

I was supposed to go back to Dublin to celebrate the release of my exam results, but when I didn't come home, and when I didn't answer the phone to him, Dad flew over to see how I was.

One Saturday morning, he found me scattering wet muesli onto the grass in Tommy's back garden, a task I approached as seriously as splitting open a new textbook.

The day was warm and perfect for sitting outside and catching up on all the news from home. Everyone was very proud of my results Dad said, and I would have to call my uncles and grandmother to tell them why I was so clever.

He was plugging me about my summer, the job, and my preparation for medical school in the autumn. I was prepared to talk to him about work, and how I was entering my final week of hauling, stacking, tending to and rolling turf and how this would likely be it for me and landscape gardening.

He wanted us to celebrate, but I said I was tired from a busy week.

But arrangements had become so loose on the site—Noel was off ('they got him,' someone said)—that I was running to an easier schedule and had barely done a thing.

We went inside and Dad settled into the chair with Tommy's jacket hanging on it—the case for *The Golden Rooftops* was in Dad's eye-line but he didn't mention it.

—Don't be thinking you're getting away without a party at home, he said.

—Do I need to be in the room while it happens?

—We can't embarrass you if you're not there, he said. The clever little head on you.

—You're talking about me like I'm some kind of little robot.

—And I'm not going to say it, Dad said.

—Please don't, I said. I'll be home soon enough. We can celebrate then. And I'll call you a lot.

—No, you won't, he said.

Dad had quite enough to go on: the more I talked about having two fry-ups every morning, and five pints at lunch with IRA men, the more I was avoiding talking about the obvious.

He found the shirt I'd bought at a second-hand place in an arcade on the Kings Road.

An old white shirt, still bright, still crisp, with dress cuffs that were just on the right side of flamboyant. What do we have here? he said, asking me how long I'd been dressing like a vagabond, which translated to: how long had I been dressing like Tommy?

My rising colour, nicely accentuated by the white shirt, was the answer.

—Bit of a soft spot for him, I take it?

—Suppose, I said.

—He has that effect on people.

I did want him to know that something more than an ordinary friendship had happened with Tommy, and I wanted to be left alone about it. Dad was trying to allow me that.

He knew what I was thinking—the world had broken open—and that his thoughts about my friendship with his cousin were irrelevant and best kept to himself.

Tommy was used to playing a role, and the person Dad and I were talking about was as much of a character as the poised young man with dubiously perfect manners and accent in *The Golden Rooftops*; or Dad's shifty young cousin who, Dad had said, did not like to be looked at let alone spoken to, and who was going to be anything but famous; or the tender lovestruck so-and-so, who would not be recognisable to anyone but me, all of which showed that Tommy wasn't one character but a number of different ones, and which showed how possessive we are of our fictions.

Of course, Dad knew him better than I ever would.

He told me about the time, about the time, about the time.

The time they been arrested for walking across a train line in a coastal Tuscan town; the time Tommy had been arrested for walking into traffic in the middle of Cologne; and the time they ran onto the pitch at Lansdowne Road, which was the time they were ejected from Lansdowne Road, and taken to cool off in the cells.

The works.

I wanted to say that Tommy had told me all of this and more.

I wanted to say that Tommy and I had done all the things Dad talked about and more.

Fuck stories, I thought, fuck them.

At the beginning, you don't have any of that, you don't have the stories, and you can't see where they join up. You don't even know it's the beginning, it's just all you have.

Dad had his Tommy, and I had mine.

Dad just had more to go on and look back on. I did

recognise Tommy in those anecdotes, surrounded and unaffected by all the chaos that followed him, but our connection was deeper and more than tales of nights out and near misses.

What's more powerful, an anecdote or a dream?

Give me a dream any day.

Anyway, I needed to tidy up, Dad said. The place was a state.

My laundry was out on the kitchen table.

I folded it up, putting some of Tommy's things in with mine.

Even after they'd been laundered and put on my bed, his bedclothes had a particular smell, and my bedroom was an inscrutable tumult of objects that had migrated from his room to mine, the tapes, glasses, sunglasses, candlesticks, socks and scarves I would have to put back, and which Dad had put together as a picture of my summer.

Dad went for a shower with some questions about dinner. He was very set on going out to eat. When he came into my room, I said, —I'll come out with you to celebrate.

—But you don't want to?

—But you want me to, I said.

The restaurant was like a schoolroom without teachers. I crossed the tiles to a table that looked too big for two people. Everyone was wearing a kind of clerical uniform.

In one of Tommy's shirts worn over my gardening

clothes, I enjoyed the fact that I must have looked like a scruff.

It was Dad's first time there, but he and the waiter were in on some prior conversation and, without asking for any, we were brought some large bottles of sparkling water, and, as I was wondering if it was okay to order a steak, Dad had just let it slip that someone had been in touch.

He might or he mightn't be back in London this weekend.

The order is unclear; I'm putting them in some kind of sequence now, but I have several versions of that moment where Tommy came to the table sideways, like he'd just slipped through a gap in a fence.

I was too used to him being away that I wasn't prepared for Tommy to be here, and for him to have become a form of gleaming reptile.

The eeriness of his skin, the paleness, and was his hair a different colour? His teeth seemed to have grown, and his eyes were big and bulging, too.

The waiter had to come and go several times.

Can you do me a nice omelette? Tommy asked him. He hadn't said anything about the fact I was wearing his shirt.

When the omelette appeared, I knew that he wouldn't eat anything. The next things he asked for were a cup of tea and a few chocolate biscuits.

I can see now that, for a while, I was gone to all that myself.

Nothing being good enough any more. Menus, jobs, families, my own family, anyone who wasn't Tommy Carmody.

Once he'd warmed up after a few glasses, Dad told Tommy about the time I'd brought notes, prompts, for a family meal.

Mum and Dad didn't really want to hear about their blood pressure at the dinner table, and they laughed, everyone laughed—not just at the little presentation but at how I had missed the point, and that I was always doing that, and on purpose, and the way I had to have things in bullet-points. The way I'd never learned to let go, or to let myself get carried away by a conversation, but insisted on beginnings, middles and ends; and, what's worse, I was right, cause this was how people are *supposed* to behave.

Then Tommy began a story that had us all believing that a drying-out clinic in Hampshire was some kind of funny ghost story.

—Giving up the drink is one thing, he said. Letting go of your freedom is another story entirely. No lock on the door, no say in what's for dinner, what time it's at. They do be in love with getting up in the middle of the night to pray and talk about themselves. But do you know why I went along with it?

—You had to? Dad said.

—I did have to, Tommy said.

The monologue that came next felt like an audition, either for my benefit or Dad's.

Pausing here and there, as if to allow for canned laughter, Tommy said he was not supposed to be working for a while, but his next job was less about the temptation to drink than the paycheque that would pay for the rehab.

—One of the nuns, he said. In her nineties, bit of a disciplinarian, that's how they made them then. Probably a bit more lenient than she was, with the encroaching years and that, and she was always staring at you, looking right through you, breakfast lunch and dinner, she'd be looking at you for so long that you just got used to her sitting up straight in her reclining chair. One day Sister Helen upped and got out of the chair, coming straight for me as I was doing my jigsaw. She had something to say to me, she said. Well, I said, would you like to say it, sister? Come with me, she said. How was I to know she could walk at all, but she took off at an awful clip. When I saw that I was to follow her to the laundry, I knew she had something up her sleeve. She opened one of the washing machines, and there was nothing in it, until she rolled the drum around and I heard the sound. Something banging around in there. A bottle of Powers stashed away. Full. Untouched. She poured us a couple of small ones, just her and me, just the two of us. I thought I'd have the one and then resume my sobriety, which was suiting me very nicely thank you. I thought that would be us, but I could tell from the way Sister Helen was with me that she wanted someone to drink with. She told me she'd remembered the day I'd arrived. I'd no idea why this was being pointed out to me, by this stage I was more interested in the whiskey, and there's nothing like the first glass of whiskey, it's golden, maybe the second one has its own way of expressing itself, too, but the first one is like listening to a beautiful ballad. It's come through the ages, and it'll keep going. These are the kinds of thoughts that were going through my head.

One poor woman who'd come to the table for an autograph got drawn into the story. She'd read Tommy was going to be in a film with Gérard Depardieu. What was he like, Depardieu?

Without hesitation, Tommy said, —A fucking fat pig.

The delivery, as you'd come to expect, was perfect. And if this person had been my world, I was lucky, I felt then, not to have known exactly what he had been going through.

—Are you ready for more? he asked. Me and Sister Helen. Someone passed by in the corridor outside the laundry door then, but they didn't come in. And it was quiet for a bit. I went to check the door, in case there was a lock on it, there wasn't, so we'd be disturbed sooner or later. I was more focused on the whiskey so that I barely noticed the woman standing there. I had to get another shot into me. It was Sister Helen at the door, not her *now* but as a young girl, and a very fine thing she was, skin as white as her habit, and all done out like a novice from *Black Narcissus*. Just in case that kind of thing does it for you. Seeing a ghost is one thing, talking to them is another, so I kept myself to myself. I got up to go but Sister Helen put her mind in mine to keep me where I was, so that she could tell me I was in the room where she used to work when she first came to the abbey. They put her to work, and that, and when she was lonely, she'd come down there, under the pretence of getting on with the laundry, and she'd have a cry and a talk to her mother, the virgin Mary, or whoever. Anyone Helen wanted to would just walk in and she'd talk to them while she was wringing sheets and putting the wet things up on the pulley, and she said if I wanted to, I could use the room myself sometimes. I could come down here and talk to whomever I wanted and see them whenever I wanted, when I needed to. And, you know, I did.

The patient way in which the Depardieu fan waited for him to sign her napkin.

—Who did you talk to? I asked.

Just in case anyone else needed an autograph, Tommy was aiming his gaze around the room. Then he put his arm on my shoulder and said he'd missed me.

These few weeks without him had had one effect on me: to represent a friendship as something that could change a person; not just your past but your plans; to live for one thing, you had to abandon the other.

When it came time to ask for the bill, I made the decision to treat them to dinner, to which Dad and Tommy whistled as one and leaned back in their chairs.

My wallet was out and not knowing otherwise, I went

up to pay, looking just like any other young man whose reason for existing was to be Tommy Carmody's dependable young friend.

All the rightness that had passed between us—getting you up in the morning and keeping you up at night—was still worth recovering.

When I turned back to the table, Tommy had a finger to his lips.

Then he held out a pale hand to shake mine.

The toothpick he handed me was wrapped in plastic, and I didn't open it (nor for years after that).

Dad asked if we'd like to walk before getting a taxi, and Tommy said we should go ahead, and he'd catch us up. Dad put his arm in mine to say that we were to let Tommy go ahead.

As he walked over to the door, I was both trying to slow his feet across the tiles and wishing him gone.

Life, now, had that tension and would continue that way.

Tommy's choice not to come back to the house, and his choice not to tell me that he wasn't coming, had been made somewhere along the way.

And I was wondering how it was, even after knowing he was the type to walk out of a place without saying where he was going, I was not the one heading off into the night with him, so that all of this wouldn't have been for nothing.

All the noise in the heart that began when I moved in with him, its secrets would make themselves known.

It may have been that Tommy Carmody was going to run and run.

He was that person in the myth who runs for ever.

City skies at night have all these alien shades of yellow and pink colours. The street was crowded and lit by cigarette and siren-lights, colours which might have come from within.

I was happy that we'd come out for dinner, and even happier still to come home to a blinking on the answering machine.

Thanks for dinner etcetera, and if I was up to making something to eat the following night, Tommy would be up to eating it.

I'd once appointed myself chef to a dinner Dad was having for some friends. This was to be no simple supper, and what plans I had: raw fish and braised game and fruit in season. It was to be important and memorable and, as far as food went, eloquent. I stuffed things with things they didn't need to be stuffed with, I stood over people to pour stuff out of a jug, I gave them a lecture about the provenance of the venison. I got in the way, and everyone was very nice, and they had to throw most of it out.

But the night was gently tilting back towards optimism.

I'd have a busy morning in the morning.

The menu to plan, a few choices to make, excitement

spiralling at the commemorative goodbyes at the end of the evening.

The lovely words we'd share, the plans we'd make.

Dad floated in quietly enough to observe me peeling spuds at the sink.

He'd been trying to talk to me about university, but any interest I had in my plans for the autumn had disappeared the moment Tommy had taken an interest in dinner.

—Give it another hour, Dad said.

—A chicken *takes* an hour, I said. We mightn't be eating till midnight.

—Very continental, Dad said.

Tommy was obviously running a bit late, and he could have been anywhere—it was enough that he was somewhere nearby, and why was it the case that people had to be off somewhere?—but I didn't want to eat without him.

—Do you think there should be a dessert? I said.

Dad said, —All I can say is that I'd love to live in a world where someone makes me dinner on a Sunday night.

We agreed on putting the food where Tommy would see it when he got in. I carved the chicken and when Igot it to the table, just about presentably, Dad greeted me with a little downturned mouth.

—I should have warned you, he said. The best way

to get him to show up for dinner is to tell him he's not invited.

—But it was his idea.

—I'm sure he meant it at the time, Dad said. But it's me who owes you an apology. I wanted this to happen, Tommy disappointing you, but I didn't want this to happen in the way that it has.

Real friendship seemed to involve hanging around and feeling sad, the joy that formed the initial equation being removed from it, and watching it disappear in slow motion.

Then Dad said, —Can I ask if you are interested in staying friends with him?

—He's an interesting person.

—And so are you. But he doesn't run to anyone's schedule but his own. Are you interested in staying in touch with him?

—Why do you keep asking that? I said. Yes, at some point, that would be the intention.

—That would be the intention? Tommy doesn't always pass other people's tests.

—I don't like testing other people.

—Yes, you do, Dad said. You'll make new friends when you get to the university, he said.

—Not necessarily one of my gifts in my life, I said.

If, as some people believed, friendship was more significant than love, for one to be true, and for it to be more than a diversion, and for it to mean anything more than companionship, it had to be one that broke, and it had to be one that ended.

Perhaps this was going to be the story of a friendship that ended.

Dad was going home in the morning. He decided we should help Tommy out by clearing some of the junk in the garden.

The sky was soft and busy, and the air was full of spinning insects. The glasshouse had those piles of newspapers, and everything else I had noticed, plus an old tandem (probably a prop taken from a film).

—We could have a go on it? Dad said.

—Let's not risk it, I said.

—You're someone who views the world as if it's in imminent danger of bursting into flames.

—Or that it already has, I said.

Dad reminded me of the first time I'd ever gone out cycling on my own. The strap of my school bag got caught in the wheels of my bike. Catastrophe. I lost a front tooth. Two halves.

—Two half catastrophes make a whole, I said.

We tidied up but decided against throwing anything out. I had been trying to keep the garden spick and span, but the end of the summer was visible as a sort of desperation in the air and the light; the light was on the move, and the softness on my father's face, and the tiredness behind his eyes, could be felt as a kind of warning.

And Tommy? What would he look like when he was

Dad's age? I wondered. His hair, what colour might it be, how might he grow it and what length would he have it?

Who was to know how life would treat someone?

Long after this summer, years from now, when I would be a doctor, all those years of wine and whiskey would have had its toll on him. Would there be any catastrophes, or half-catastrophes? But someone like Tommy Carmody would know how to manage that, and the longer you lived the smarter you got.

So it was that I was able to imagine how he might seem in twenty, thirty, forty years, just not if I would know him then, and or if I would ever get to behold it.

I went up to bed. Would I come down in the morning to find Tommy in the kitchen?

Eating everything I'd left out on the table. Waiting with an apology like a handful of wildflowers just picked from the garden.

I'd wear his shirt to sleep in tonight, and know what it meant to be him, open to the truth of the world, as open as he was when he'd go away.

Not to leave life but to get closer to it.

His bedroom door, which I always made a point of keeping shut, was open to reveal the lamp on by the bed. Perhaps Dad had been in there to get something, and I stood uncertainly by the door to listen. In that tense and tender silence, I could just about hear Tommy's voice from before.

Can you please close the door?

I'd like to be alone.

You Know Who

2004

Light a candle, put it out, kneel down, sit down, stand up, sing, sing in tune, walk in a circle, never the same one twice, serve the guests, clear the table, get more Flora, check the readings, see about getting some of those rubber Birkenstocks, question the firmness of your skull, recite the psalms, do them again, add one in, skip one out, approach the altar, wait your turn, remember that it's chocolate milk on Tuesdays, dress the altar, bow from the waist, waggle your toes, don't speak but speak in your heart.

We busied ourselves with work and prayer.

There was wonder and release to be had in the days.

—What's a dough-ball?

—You know dough? she said. A ball of that.

—But cooked?

—Cooked.

—Crusty?

—A bit softer, kind of like a doughnut.

—So it's sweet? I said.

—I shouldn't have said doughnut, she said. Different type of dough.

—What's the dip?

—It's dip, she said. It's wetter than the dough.

This was Dublin at the beginning of the century. Servers in a pizza place had more to deal with than someone's confusion at the concept of dipping food into other foods.

I didn't have the dough balls, but they were amused to find a man with rosary beads in a denim work-smock interested in ordering a Fiorentina.

This was the one with the egg.

Egg on a pizza.

If not quite at the level of believing in a benevolent deity, it was another concept that needed explaining at length.

When my clothing didn't announce me as a man of the cloth, my table manners did. It's a civilised life, but monks live in the company of You Know Who, and it's no surprise that they forget themselves when they eat.

We'd eat in silence, with one of the brothers reading to us. When someone doesn't talk much (they can't or they won't or they're not allowed to), either they can go in on themselves, or they become expressive in other ways.

Just as you get to know the names of pizzas, you can grow to be a connoisseur of silence.

There was companionable silence.

There was meaningful silence.

There were uproarious, gusty silences.

I knew there were dreadful silences.

And sweet silence, and still silence.

But there would be cattle on the hill, work going on in the woodshed, and there was very rarely total silence.

From the first time I saw him, I was struck by the fact that the abbot, Father Ambrose, walked the way a monk was supposed to walk. He could get from one place to another without seeming to move himself at all.

Sometimes his stoop seemed to weigh on him and some days he carried it with a swing.

The way he hauled air as he gave a blessing.

He had a very articulate way of moving.

I often think of the first time I saw him ring the bells before vespers, working the ropes like he was throttling someone, and the bells singing out so finely. I found myself following him around, trying to decipher something from the depth of his genuflection or why he'd lean one way or another to allow you to pass, or the angle at which he carried his cup and plate across the refectory.

Our supper in the winter was usually Weetabix. In the summer, it would be cheese and biscuits with salad from the gardens. Most of us would take our plates to the sideboard but Ambrose carried handfuls of leaves back to his place at the table, as though he'd just picked them.

Some answers to frequently asked questions:

Monks are very hands-on when it comes to practical matters, but they are not oblivious to comfort.

Life in the monastery is not as pleasureless as you might expect, and monks do get sad, sometimes, almost petulant, especially if lunch hasn't been good or it hasn't been made and served with care.

They look forward to lunch.

These things matter.

I ate the pizza—not the only one to be using my hands—and considered another. The first one was on the modest side, and it was plain that I would not be back here any time soon.

After eating, I prayed for a while as the servers cleaned around me.

The wedding I was officiating at was the next day, and there was no hurry.

There is never any hurry.

Before he'd dropped me at the Shelbourne and told me that the room and breakfast was taken care of, the best man had given me two hundred euro for walking-around money.

And walking around town earlier, in tasteful pink light, on newly manicured pavements, I was admiring the newfound tastefulness of the buskers, and admiring the tasteful people admiring the buskers, and admiring the people admiring the people admiring the buskers, and totally, totally, totally wasn't being overwhelmed at being back in Dublin after nearly ten years away.

I don't have a scene for you, or much of an instance, or even a moment, but at some point, over the next fifteen years, You Know What had become You Know Who.

Or perhaps something had happened to remind me how empty I'd been feeling.

In the mid-nineties, I was a junior doctor in Glasgow.

Every fortnight the medical faculty at the university invited a guest-speaker to spend time with the students.

Mr Tom Wurdmann, a consultant who worked with rugby players and their lower backs, was no more or less boring than anyone else who'd been in to visit us. I was starting to notice a pattern in my classmates, who were more interested in each other and only in what rugby players and their neurologists got paid. Only I was taking notes, and only I asked Mr Wurdmann anything—taking care to make a meal of the question. Fifty billion proteins per neuron? Really? Mr Wurdmann dealt with this nimbly but, sensing that would be it for questions, pivoted into a lecture's worth of material on genes and proteins. More murmuring. Imagine that, he said, but no one did. There was the sound of a door closing, all collective curiosity departing with the first person with the nerve to leave the classroom. It was the same when Mr Wurdmann invited the students for ice-cream as his guests. It took about thirty seconds to clear the room. When I went up to say thank you for the talk, and to say that I had to get home to study, the poor man looked like he was about to cry.

Mr Wurdmann wanted to go somewhere and had no one to go with, and I wanted to go somewhere and had no one to go with, and we both went our separate ways. I knew lonely when I saw it.

The next day, I walked out of a hospital in the middle of a sixty-hour day. I got on a train leaving for the Highlands, where I got on another train across the Highlands, and from there I walked two hours in some warm, sweet rain.

All I know is that my heart had been in an iron clamp, and this was how it was going to be.

No Mum.

Clamp around your heart.

No Mum.

Ghost in your head.

No Mum.

Ghost in your chest.

Getting to the abbey just as the brothers were finishing work for the afternoon, I was so drenched that the first monk I met, Brother Michael Anthony, was amused to hear that I was just there to learn about apples.

The orchard ascended towards an expanse of grass big enough for a racecourse. It was the time of year when the earth comes into itself, and the trees were buoyant and beautiful in their postures. In all their variety, they looked very sure of themselves, except for one tree I could have pulled out of the ground with my two arms. The other ones were oily with good health, but its leaves were less lustrous, and the fruit was nothing to speak of this far into the summer.

Michael Anthony didn't reply when I pointed this out.

Eventually he said that the wind blew through its leaves just as much as the others.

The orchard, being his main project in life, gave us more to talk about. He walked me through some Joy Bells, Golden Nobles, Ribston Pippins, William Crumps. White Melrose and Tower of Glamis. They had some in storage—the main crop hadn't come into its own yet—and when he asked if I wanted some to take with me, it was Michael Anthony's way of asking how long I was planning on staying and when I was planning on going.

He was an old man, very tall and very fit, and I was welcome to join him for a quick tour of the orchard. If I was hungry he could arrange for me to have supper with the monks, which might have been a punishment more than a kindness, he said, since it was Brother William's turn at the soup, and conceptually what I might eat could be counted as soup (potatoes, theirs; leeks, theirs; water, everyone's) but William seemed to have it in for the concept of food in its entirety.

An hour or two later I was committing the sin of breaking the silence at supper by complementing them all on their cooking and offering to clear up and do the dishes.

Towards nightfall the sun made a modest show from behind the hill, brightening them from within. Once I'd seen Ambrose blessing the brothers at compline, I knew I would not be able to sleep right until I'd received that release at the end of a day.

The scrubbing of tiles and the pans, the doing of the laundry, all the processing in and out to the chapel, this helped in sticking to the path, but nothing worked better than prayer.

Sometimes the heart won't settle.

And when the spirit would come to me at night, it did so only to say how difficult it might be to find. The heat inside, I prayed it away, but prayer takes practice, and it isn't unusual to feel like you are getting away with it.

I soon gained an understanding of how you can appear peaceful to yourself; you can deliberate over every gesture—chin to chest, genuflect—and you can still look up and the room is on fire.

It's not as if there is ever a fire.

It's not as if we ever have to do anything.

Fill a bucket, run a hose, descend on a rope; although all of these things could be true.

Perhaps, when we pray, we call upon the impossible.

Occasionally it will relent with an answer.

My father hadn't been replying to my letters. I was allowed to send one a week, and after a while you do prefer to write to someone who'll reply.

Dad was a wine merchant and at first there were jokes about the quality of the stuff in the chalices, but the jokes thinned out and the letters thinned out. It was one thing for my father to object to me becoming a monk, another to close the hand of friendship altogether.

When Mum got sick, she discovered her faith, turning away from me and my father; as if there could be only the one source of love in her life: You Know Who.

Not long before I got on that train to the Highlands, I wrote to Dad to say that life wasn't quite right without her and more and more I was forgetting what my mother's love felt like, and what love felt like.

Well, Dad wrote. Well, well.

My letter was very lovely, but it had missed the point. Saying something isn't right is not the same as it being all wrong.

The abbot would not have needed to know that I was being put up in a five-star hotel. The Shelbourne wasn't what you might call to his taste, but Ambrose did not know, and I wasn't going to tell him.

The wedding was going to be in the Sacred Heart in Donnybrook and the reception, and all its tomfoolery, was going to be at the hotel. My friends Rory and Nuala, the bride and groom, were talking as if the afters would have to be navigated like some kind of crash landing.

The Alaska Airlines flight disappearing into the Pacific.

The receptionist, who wanted me to know that she was called Denice with a small c, and, I supposed, a big D, seemed to know all about me. The bridal party had indicated that I was a VVIP, and Denice was happy to let slip that a Buddhist high lama had just been staying in one of the suites and they'd got sheep's curd in for his breakfast.

—The bridal party said you were a fun priest, she said. It's our job to get the VVIPs everything they need.

—I'm sure clear you do that exceptionally well, I said.

She handed me my room key and told me I was welcome to join everyone in the bar. The drinks, including Champagne, were paid for.

My friend Rory Butler wouldn't have conceived of a wedding in which Champagne wasn't included and never-ending. In the years after school, indulgences and temptation, and debt, followed him around like an eager girlfriend.

—And is there anything else you need? Denice said.

—Nothing at all, I said.

—Well, that's boring, she said.

When I asked if there was anything I could do to help about the place, I was told that everything was taken care of, and that I would be well advised to cross the lobby and get started on some of that Champagne.

I reminded Denice that my every wish was to be granted.

A minute or two later, once she had had it explained to her, I was helping a nice cleaner called Martina do the downstairs bathrooms.

I was in the gents, concentrating not on the job in hand—the toilets were spotless—and not on what I might have been doing back at the monastery, cutting a hedge, and not on the brisk, officious sound of someone taking drugs in a cubicle along from mine. I was thinking we should all do this occasionally. It didn't have to be in the Shelbourne Hotel.

In their afternoons, after lunch and perhaps a little sleep, there was always something for the monks to do. Work could be manual, the glories of weeding, or it could be an administrative task like taking photographs of the honey to put up on the website.

It's not work if it's done for little or no money.

It's not work if it's done for the glory and satisfaction of others.

It's not work if it's done with a full heart.

It's not work if you don't do the work.

Knock on the neighbour's door, ask to clean their toilets.

Ask if they need anything done in the garden, ask to

take out the bins, mow the lawn, fix the mower, get them one if they don't have one. It's something I still do from time to time, and once you get over the funny looks, the good feelings you can access and the goodness you can share in, it is so simple, the act of doing something for someone else.

It can be so simple that you barely think to do it.

The lobby in the Shelbourne had two lounges and two bars, and I was drawn towards the bigger bar that faced onto Dawson Street, partly cause no one in that room had any interest in what was going on outside it.

I've been in plenty of bars and, quiet or busy, they all have one thing in common.

No one listens.

Conversation is a sport where you position yourself to accumulate points. The chats going on in the side bar may have been as tactical as any; but this, as far as I could see, was a room flushed by all the promise that we conceive of on the night before a wedding: every table a game of musical chairs, gents heading for the ladies and ladies heading for the gents, the certain redemption of another tray of pints, the promise kept topped up at a certain level.

I got as far as the doorway.

Someone with Guinness cream in his lips came out with some pints on a tray. —How's the form, Ian? he said.

I'd no idea who he was, and I couldn't really stand there any longer without staying or going.

There was the sound of song from somewhere and I followed it across the lobby to the Horseshoe bar tucked away in the corner, drawn there partly cause I was nervous about going to my room.

On one hand, it was going to be interesting to spend the night in a double bed and to be sleeping past four in the morning—which I wouldn't do anyway, if only cause I liked to keep my routines.

Vigils.

Lectio divina.

Lauds.

Pittance.

Prime.

Mass.

Terce.

Work.

Sext.

Lunch.

Meridian.

None.

Work.

Vespers.

Prayer.

Chapter.

Compline.

The great silence of the night.

All of this helped me account for my existence and regulate it.

At the monastery guesthouse, we were used to dealing

with those who couldn't sleep at all. Our windows looked out onto the same dark forest, and beyond it the great nothing.

What else could we do but sing for our people and pray for them? That's what they came to us for. I also stripped their beds and emptied their wastepaper baskets.

All in the name of love.

How many people were squeezed into that little bar?

Third-class travel with first-class prices.

Faces peering out, but no one here appeared to be drinking Champagne, and I wasn't sure if this room belonged to the wedding party or not.

The last time I'd been in a pub had been before the smoking ban. The smells were certainly more organic than before. A brave new world with the same old smells. What this place needed was some incense.

A singer in a woolly hat sat on a stool at one side of the little horseshoe.

The two or three people along from her had their eyes closed, and others around the room were sitting up straight with their bellies held in. She was singing 'Óró Mo Bháidín', one rendition after another.

Perhaps it was the only song everyone there knew.

I will raise the sails, as she glides in the bay.

But these were very strange versions, the melody drifting towards an abrasiveness I could feel in my chest. Eventually, on the third or fourth go-around, the singer found a pitch that got the room on her side, and everyone became still. After another verse or two, some of the others began to join in sweetly, everyone going in their own direction.

The accompaniment was frighteningly enthusiastic and particularly bad and, when the song finished, the applause rose up like a wind, allowing the room to return to its liveliness, the spoken voices knitting together better than the sung ones.

Tommy Carmody was right in front of me.

A few different drinks were being tended to, none of them very carefully. If he was just on the edge of sobriety, it looked like he was paying attention to nothing much.

Then his face lightened.

When he put a finger to his lips, all I could do was act normal.

I suppose he'd known I was there all along.

The last time I'd seen him, Tommy was one of the more high-minded characters on a TV drama about MI6 agents on a dangerous mission. He'd worn horn-rimmed glasses and a pinstripe suit that did wonders for his shoulders.

He was not like that now. The beard made him look like a wolfhound.

The woman next to him—whose way of dressing was more ecclesiastical than my own—still had her eyes closed from the song but Tommy was deep in conversation with her anyway.

Having become a noticer of these things, I'd have to have seen them up close, but her trousers looked like they'd been made with a top stitch.

The monks make their own clothes, and Michael Anthony had been teaching me to cut and sew. It was all too much at first—I couldn't picture a roll of cloth as anything more than that—but I'd been looking at taking over from him in the workshop. Starting with the scapulars, which were as easy as cutting out an apron; I was almost immobilised with excitement the first I time I mastered the pleat in a cowl.

Without taking his eye off his neighbour, the nearly-nun, Tommy called out my name, like he was asking me to get something for him.

The tone was quite sharp. He was either impatient with the wait for me to notice him, or with the conversation he was in, and it was the effort of distinguishing one form of annoyance from another that was causing the most annoyance.

The woman beside him was being asked to shove along and, with a quick look my way, Tommy patted the seat beside him. As I made my way over there, he then began pointing madly behind me.

No, Tommy was pointing a few feet to the other side of me.

Only the waggling glass in his other hand got his point across.

He needed a pint.

Of all the things that had happened today, being sent

to the bar before we had even said hello was the least surprising.

When I first met Tommy, I could be embarrassed by a sharp word, a kind word. Hello, goodnight, the offer of a cup of tea, someone—Tommy Carmody was that someone—making breakfast. Then and now, I could be embarrassed by someone singing for me, a melody, the way it would break and then fall away and be gone, and I'd be so attached it, and that would be embarrassing, too.

Nor was there any need to call for the pint, the barman had one on, and by the time I reached his table, Tommy had resumed his conversation with the nearly-nun.

He had begun a small part as Conchobar mac Nessa, the bad husband, in a movie called *Maeve, Queen of Connacht.*

Somehow, he had been passed over for a role in the film Steven Soderbergh had just made in Dublin, and he was waiting to hear about a Christmas movie being filmed in Wicklow, doubling as Lapland, and the biopic of Charles Stewart Parnell he'd been attached to for about twenty years had just about closed its financing. All the beards he'd grown and shaved in anticipation of production money being about to arrive.

The trouble with acting, Tommy said, is that you were always waiting for permission.

But he loved the life very much. It was one of the great privileges in a person's life to get into the back of any vehicle that pulled up at your front door.

The pint arrived to the warmest of greetings.

All through this he fielded greetings, goodbyes, making detailed arrangements with passersby—with whom he hadn't spoken all evening—that none of them, surely, had any intention of fulfilling.

The nearly-nun next to him was his wife.

The three of us were positioned like objects painted into a still life at different times. Not quite apart, not quite together.

Tommy hadn't introduced us, except to say that her name was Petra and that she was in finance and that didn't seem to matter.

While Tommy knew I was to be one of the celebrants at Rory's wedding the next day, of all the things he was interested in about me, my faith and my way of life, the demands it made on me and what it gave me, did not seem to come into it.

We talked for an hour, more, about someone who took a packed lunch to a building site, the clever and clueless boy with all that curiosity about midnights and dawns, which had never been satisfied. (I have prayed through thousands of dawns since then.) And still we kept the conversation going, talking in the way we always had; always something unrelated to the previous thread in the way that a fallen tree relates to a storm that has long since passed on.

As the night wore on, Tommy became interested in the fact that, as a resident at the hotel, one of my privileges would be to move us all into the Lord Mayor's lounge and order drinks into the night.

—Order away, I said.

—Don't might if I do, he said. I need to unwind. I'm in tatters, here. Queen Maeve would tear the arse out of anyone.

But the pints were landing at a slower pace, and the singers were moving on and arrangements were made to meet in the morning.

Petra had left with them, and we had the little bar to ourselves.

I was permitted by Tommy to offer him a last drink, a Black Bush, and only when it was the two of us did he really seem to recognise that it was me. But he'd known to call me Eugene and not Ian.

He said, —Where are the robes? I was expecting robes.

—Tomorrow, I said.

—We all love you, Brother Eugene, you're amazing, whatever it is you're doing, you believe in it, so I believe in it. So, last one, before we go for the night. Do your eyes ever deceive you?

—Not often.

—Do you see him?

—Do I *see* him?

—Like you've been out on the tear for a few days, and you've come home, and the telly has gone on the blink, and you don't know if it's you or the TV. Your eyes are playing tricks on you.

My certainty was that I was shaped by experience to be lonely.

—I'm not myself without him, no.

—Jaysuz, that was quick, he said.

Each night, the monastery has its great silence. The great stillness, the great anticipation, the great trepidation, the great prolongation, the great perturbation, the restlessness, hopelessness, uselessness, the waiting and wondering.

The great mystification, the great bewilderment, the great loneliness.

The loneliness came more often when you were unawares.

We sat quiet, then, Tommy and I.

Him, certain in his incomprehension.

Me, attempting to resolve the irresolvable, which is one thing a monk should never do (although this is all some of us ever did).

—I might as well be talking to an empty seat, he said.

—I'm here, I said.

—You can't be in two places at once. We're all searching for something, right? I'm at the same thing. I can hold my own, I'm out there, too. But there's a spark on this shoot, Terry, and I like to have lunch with them lads, just to see what's going on in the world; they're more out there than you and me put together. Out where the buses don't go. Fell off a scaffold once and one of his ribs came out his mouth. Back at work first thing in the morning. And Terry asked me why I was so quiet, all the time. Thinking, I said, having my deep thoughts. Deep thoughts? Terry said. Deep thoughts. He's never had a thought in his life.

—It's not *about* thinking, I said.

I had never told Tommy that I thought of him every day and that all the time since we'd seen each other had passed as a very long kind of prayer. I might have shared this with him now, but he had done his talking for the night.

Just as he was ruminating on the idea of another small one for the road, Petra came to tell Tommy their car was waiting.

I was left alone in the bar with one thought.

A good friendship gives you bearings.

It can be used in the way that a wristwatch can act as a makeshift compass, the hour hand pointing towards the sun, the imaginary line pointing south and, if Tommy Carmody had been my imaginary line, if I could wait, I could now see which way it was moving, I could find the sun.

The imaginary line that had been passing between us tonight.

And it had made no sense at all, being away from him this long.

We'd run into each other once since 1989. A sunny morning in north London, as I always remember it being when we met.

I'd been in Tottenham for a noviciate's retreat, and was, on a whim, visiting the cemetery in Highgate. Tommy had been shooting a film being made from a screenplay by Guy Ritchie's accountant's cousin.

Awful muck, he said, but the cultural conversation must be followed where it wants to go.

The scene they were making in the cemetery was the one in which his character got sliced from head to toe by an assailant dressed as a milkman.

We chatted before he had to go back to work, and we made an arrangement for a swim on Hampstead Heath once the retreat had wound up. A week in the rarefied company of St Benedict, fount of all regularity, essential admin for the spirit.

There was a part of me that ended up not being there.

In a few days, I would be in Tommy's orbit. In a few days the better, funnier part of my being would be shaken awake.

And Tommy would know none of my fear and excitement. Nor did he take much account of the fact that I had lied to the abbot to spend a few more days in London.

I was just about to take my temporary vows. Well on the way to being a monk, then, another remnant from the human patchwork, the kind of spiritual runaway and lost soul that only a mother could understand.

Monks wear dresses.

They levitate.

They spend days doodling on manuscripts.

They don't speak. They get up in the middle of the night (the last one is true). They'll be ex-junkies, right-wing zealots, left-wing ones, brain dead, or brainwashed in one way or another.

If this is what you hear, it's not who I was.

When I explained this to Tommy as he was getting down to his swimming togs, the apprehensive way in which he regarded the water said one thing.

Blah-blah Jesus.

In all the time we spent together, we'd sidle into conversation in the same way I was entering the water Tommy had just flung himself into.

The rhythms were well established. We always got there in the end.

It wasn't until we were both in the water that Tommy was ready to talk.

We were floating close by a trio of women—one who had just disentangled herself from a thirty-year marriage, and who had difficulty in floating and talking simultaneously, another with a swimming cap with angel's wings on it, the other one with skin as impressive as fresh lacquer—and by the time we were safely away from them, and Tommy could splutter a few words that weren't curses, there was the increased likelihood of there being a frank exchange between us.

Blah-blah Jesus.

It could have been the temperature of the water—and I assumed Tommy was always in some way hungover—but the words were quicker and sharper than any we'd ever had.

—I couldn't sleep last night, he said. I was thinking about you. Leaving the world behind. I always pictured you as a family man, buckets and spades, estate cars, roof racks. I don't mean anything bad here, and it's perfectly normal to be looking for something more. Change the fucking subject, entirely. Rearrange the furniture, go macrobiotic or something. I'd like my life to be different, too, but I'd rather you just weren't in there. With them.

—I understand, I said.

—I don't think you do, Tommy said.

I'm not a good swimmer, I was having a hard time staying afloat, but I wanted to stay there long enough to say, —Tell me, I'm listening.

—We need our best men in the world. Contributing.

—I am contributing.

—Tell me, he said. I'm listening.

—I have nothing better to do, I said.

—That's an answer.

—I just don't see there is a better way to spend my life.

—It just doesn't compute, he said. There's so much good life you're cutting yourself off from.

Getting in a friend's way was a brave, and perhaps generous, thing to do. But I wanted Tommy to answer one question: weren't we both smart enough to accommodate an existence that doesn't make perfect sense?

If Tommy had really wanted to push the computing thought, we could have cajoled a very revealing graph from the night of the roast chicken until now.

School, university, work, monastery, this.

Adjustment, adjustment, adjustment, adjustment.

Tommy's own graph would have been very wavy indeed.

At least his questions were made from a different flavour than my father's.

One said you can't, the other said you can.

One said stop, the other said think about it.

One said no, the other said please.

Even so, when I had just arrived at the monastery, I wrote Tommy a long letter describing my daily routine. It was all so new and exciting to me that perhaps I'd gone into too much detail. But not wanting to dig into anything too liturgical, I did mention the peace, in the north transept at night, in my little cell, and in the gardens anytime.

It wasn't the custom for the monks to talk while we worked.

There was no need to talk. We were there to listen.

Our work was a perfect expression of our love for the world.

Brother This would look after the apples but didn't eat any, Brother That liked his apples in a pie, and Brother The Other ate his with a penknife. Michael Anthony, of course, did the research on all the varieties, liked to do the clean-up and all the pruning, and it was he who prepared all the organic treatments—the copper, and the neem oil—for the trees. This arrangement suited me, and I fitted myself in around the others. Now and then I did get under someone's feet, and I'd take myself off to the kitchen garden, where, at first, Brother Gabriel was troubled by any offers of help but when he got used to me—this took months—and kept the chat to a minimum, he'd bustle around me, handing me a trowel and a packet of seeds, and the feeling of satisfaction that came with helping the vegetables along surpassed even all my excitement around the apples.

The vegetable garden peaked in midsummer and the fruit came into its own in the autumn, all of it going together as nicely as a dance; so I also drew Tommy a map of the orchard, in which I had attempted to capture the different trees. Thinking drawing pictures of apple trees to be a bit much, I had carried the letter with me for weeks before posting it. I was certain that my enthusiasm for this new life was too vivid and private to share.

It turns out that it was.

Tommy's reply, a few months later, came with a postmark from somewhere in South America. All very lovely, it said, you're setting a fine scene, but what do you want me to say in return?

This was the Tommy I was contending with now.

I had made this mistake with him before, thinking I was special.

It was a strange night spent spinning my wheels. Starched pillowcases are lost on me, and I'd hardly been able to hear my heart over the noise of the sheets.

I laid awake until dawn, staying in my clothes, as I often do, now and then perking up at the kinds of hotel comings and goings excitingly alien to anyone who lived in a monastery.

A shower with the hotel soap and shampoo that reminded me of my mother and the little tray of perfumes on her dressing table.

I am comfortable with feelings I can't name, but there is one I can't let go of, and it was attached to her smell: a person's skin, lovely and clean, and that was as far as I went, cause that is as far as I ever go.

And I thought, if I'm ever to be with someone, will they see how inadequate I am? If I'm ever to be with someone, will they see how scared I am?

There was one of the balmiest, brightest dawns for my walk to the church in the morning. The light was soft and spotty and the trees on Stephen's Green swayed so cheerily that I had to stifle a thank you to them.

It's hard to describe something you do every day for years. But faith was won or lost by the way you went about recovering the spirit before mass. Often, it had gone away. You were feeling crazy in yourself, and you were supposed to go out there and speak the word of You Know Who.

It did take a bit of figuring out and my thoughts were often so dense and immovable that it would take a talking-to to get my spirit in tune with proceedings.

What were monks there for?

To dole out the Eucharist, to chew on our quills?

We existed to listen, to ourselves and others.

We prayed, and through this prayer we activated souls, ours and others'.

We spoke for the voiceless.

We named the nameless.

We found lost things, past lives, memories, and we looked after them. If we were put here to do all that, sometimes the spirited departed.

The walk took nearly an hour, and even at an easy pace, it took some work to dissolve all the half-thoughts (Ambrose and Tommy were having a right old go at it in my mind) and it wasn't until I was all the way along Leeson Street that it all began to melt away.

By the time I got to Donnybrook, the spirit was showing its usual willing.

It helps that churches are made from good materials, and this sacristy had that sense of permanence to it.

Vestments can seem borrowed, and the vestments for a wedding are like an embroidered bedsheet, but these ones sat quite well. I didn't have to do anything but smooth them down and work my way into the morning.

One of Rory's uncles, an important bishop in Limerick, was the main celebrant. The vesting prayers were whispered as we dressed, to show respect for one another and cause there is a special way of being just before saying mass.

I have often wondered what it would be like to walk in off the street and say mass without any preparation. How much build-up would you need? Ten to fifteen minutes, or your whole life, was Ambrose's usual response.

The altar was being prepared and there was a trace of those soapy incense smells I find so comforting.

Our abbey at dawn had an aroma that I will never get over.

There is the proximity of earth and stone first of all, and the wildness of the air in that part of the world. Sometimes there are burning logs, fallen in our own forest, or the liveliness of spores after rain.

No candle can compete with that.

It hadn't turned into the best of weathers, but the clouds above the church had just become more defined, their edges etched in silver.

I followed Rory's uncle out to greet the guests. It may have been unseemly to get one of the people officiating at your wedding in a headlock, but this was a day operating from its own energy source.

When Rory took me around the car park, it was a little like being a dog at Crufts. Nothing to do but transmit the serenity they'd be expecting from me.

Perhaps he had planned this, or perhaps she had just popped into his eyeline, but Rory was now dragging me past so many old friends—people I wanted to see, the past is often friendlier than you think—to find Rosemary Walton.

He'd gone looking for her.

—I'm going to leave you pair to it, he said. Rosemary, you do the talking. Don't ask Ian what's under his robes.

I'd heard Rosemary Walton was with someone and then I heard she wasn't and when I asked Rory to stop telling me anything, it was not for fear that I'd ever stray from my path but from the sense that everything has its time and ours had gone.

Which was not to say that I never thought about her.

—Are you okay with this? she said. You stuck your head into the bar last night. I was trying to get your attention. You were as well avoiding us. We were on a mission. Staying in that expensive hotel and all I could eat for breakfast was toast. And now I can't believe I'm wittering on to a monk about toast.

—We all need our daily bread, I said.

—Do you *bake* now, Ian? This gets better.

—It's Brother Eugene, and I do, as it happens. If we want to have bread, someone has to make it.

—No shops, no? It'd be just like me to start talking about communion now.

She lived in Toronto now, where she worked as an assistant to an associate of the woman who had discovered Margaret Atwood, but cause everyone was coming back to Dublin she was coming back, too.

We had not spoken since the end of school, but she had kept up with my movements through Rory, so it felt like we'd stayed in touch. The year we'd spent going out was a time of life that circled in my mind but I never fully returned to; there was still too much possibility attached to it.

She did want to know about the robes, everyone did.

Our school shoes, she remembered, had helped set us apart from everyone else. Her ballet slippers had been ahead of their time, and my Jesus sandals, even in our school days, were something to behold.

Out went her foot, and she took a photo on her phone of her feet beside mine.

—Are you on your own? she said. Although monks don't exactly bring dates to weddings, do they? I left my boyfriend in Toronto. Old boyfriend. In a hurry. We were engaged. And then we weren't.

—Was that in a hurry too? I said.

—No. That took a long time. Four years. Break. On again. Four years. Break. On again. I sound like the World Cup! Long time, anyway. Now I'm about to move back with my parents. Against their will, more or less. And I'm a hundred times funnier when I'm not trying to be funny.

The area around her neck, and just below it, which there's a word for, was always very revealing of her mood, and I couldn't look at it now.

Even thinking that way was one good reason for me to get back to the sacristy.

We arranged to talk more at the reception, by which time I'd be back from a walk around town, and I'd have used my walking-around money to buy some souvenirs for the brothers, after which perhaps I'd end the day with some more time with Tommy, as if that hadn't been the entire point of the trip.

It's not that I ever went through the motions during mass. We abstract ourselves to get closer to You Know Who, and You Know Who can certainly tire of our messing around.

There were moments during that wedding where I may as well have been standing in the vegetable aisle at Tesco, staring at out-of-season aubergines. Now and then I saw how absorbed Rory and Nuala were in one another.

At the moment where they exchanged vows, she held out a hand behind his back, and Rory took it in a way that said he'd expected it to be there.

And I'd been keeping an eye out for someone of my own. I wasn't so distracted from what I was doing with the offertory, but I did know where Tommy was.

The tension of performing tasks that you go about habitually, wordlessly, but now under a line of observation. Delivering the prayers for the faithful, I caught that bead of light between us.

My hesitation between lines of the prayer said: do you see me?

He saw me.

And how frail and pale he looked now.

I'd noticed this more in the pictures I'd seen lately. Less cheek, more beard, less lustre in the hair. He'd put it down to the weight loss for the new role, the stresses of playing a bad man.

He was looking about himself, too—this was not a wedding in which his was the best-known face but, in that lightning nod, Tommy was handing over more of the power he had always given.

His presence in church opened up the rest of the day,

and to speak of love that day is to speak of ripening, tender love of any kind. When I took the chalice from the bishop at the beginning of communion, I saw him somewhere to the back of the queue.

Strange to see Tommy Carmody so docile, shuffling along. Typical to be the only one looking miserable at a wedding. Petra was behind him, completely impassive, too. They deserved their privacy and the moment where I presented him with the Eucharist was over with so fast that afterwards I had to wipe my face with my sleeve.

As soon as he'd had communion, Tommy left the church.

Then Rory took control of the moment.

This is something he has always done so well. The same guy who'll apply for planning permission to raze a children's playground will look at a beautiful picture like the closing moments of his own wedding ceremony and say, yes, I can build on that.

This legendary occasion can always handle a little more.

He was shaking as he walked towards Nuala.

I don't think anyone had known anything about a song. Maybe the idea to sing had just come over him, I hoped that it had, and if you'd been searching for its existence, love was out there in the flow from Petra to Rosemary to faces from the newspapers, old teachers and neighbours.

I've heard 'Forever Young' sung at many a funeral, but Rory made it into a courting song, a song for everyone there. After a murmur, and a collective sigh, like the noise made at the sight of an acrobat at a circus, harmonies began to appear from around the room.

I wanted the song to go on and on, but Rory might have collapsed, standing there, looking so desperately and softly around him. His nerves only gave the words more force, and when he was finished, Nuala took him by the hand and dragged him through a little dance, all to quiet approval from his uncle on the altar.

The church might as well have been empty, quiet as a bedroom.

Nuala was telling Rory he'd done really, really well.

On with the business of the day, which could not have been staged better if I'd come dressed as a Morris dancer or a clown.

My fair share of funny comments, my fair share of admiring looks, one or two unpleasant ones (like children who'd come out to throw stones at an invader's tank), each interaction running for approximately ninety seconds, and involving people who were dying to say so much hardly ever saying a thing.

I knew to make it about the other person.

Monks can exist as a person's reflection.

They get used to people's reactions.

People staring as you wait for your prescription.

People staring as you load the trolley at the cash and carry with catering packs of pickle. You could see them assembling their thoughts, as if seeing a monk brings on a reckoning of the soul. But not every conversation has to end in a homily. Some monks would rather talk about who won Wimbledon.

But we had well-practised moves: bow the head, turn the mouth, put some gentleness in the stride. Each had its own part of the message, which was: there's nothing to be afraid of.

Tommy was observing proceedings from a seat at the top of the staircase in the lobby. I went up to him, accepting his toast with an exaggerated genuflection.

—Join me for a drink, he said.

The tired side of him was to be expected, but the intake from the night before, and however many nights before that, and the gusto of the servers (at Rory's behest) would have unhinged a Viking.

—If you like, I said.

—If you *like*? he said. Take a walk with me. Let's show you off to people. You were great earlier. Very regal, very otherworldly. Glad I got to see the robes.

—I was about to get changed.

—Lap of honour, first, he said.

We headed down to the lobby, Tommy taking my arm with the instruction that this was a master-shot and, in these kinds of scenes, there was no distinction between actors and extras.

We were to walk and talk as if everyone and everything was in frame.

—I'm not sure I can handle the pressure, I said.

—Just pretend, he said.

There was a stirring when we entered the Lord Mayor's Lounge, some of that down to the fearsome picture of Tommy Carmody as Conchobar mac Nessa that had just leaked online. At least this wasn't the first century BC and he wasn't walking around the Shelbourne with a vicious wound in his head.

I took in all that could be taken in, but it was more that I was walking with Tommy Carmody, and he had chosen to walk with me.

At his presence, one of the managers scooted over to remove a reserved sign from a corner table. Even by her invisible insistence, the cushions on the chairs fattened themselves and the curtains inched back to offer more of a view of the passersby who were more interested in looking in at us.

Tommy was sticking with the theme of the day. —Tell me something, he said. What's love?

—Can't we begin with an easier one? I said.

—Love is? Go! First answer. You're going to say You Know Who, aren't you?

—I was going to, I said.

—No comment, he said. Just pretend you're walking around a room like this. And you've had the few pints but not too many. There's a bar full of people you can talk to, and nobody you really want to avoid, and the people you can talk to, you can get right into it, they'll answer my question. They might even rephrase it. Where is love? is a better question.

These were the first clouds of despair, although it's true

that I may not have noticed them before now. To think of Tommy ever having truly desolate moments—too devoted to my devotion, I'd forgotten about those.

Devotion can collapse denial and not noticing into one another.

Back in the lobby, Tommy directed us to the bar I'd been so quick to escape the night before.

When we'd made our tour of the room (it was humming), he pulled the barman aside and, with little more than a whisper, we were provided with stools, Tommy's phone was put on to charge, and he had jumped the queue for one of the settling pints.

From these, the best seats in the house, it wasn't difficult to see the pronounced ways in which we apply ourselves to abandon. How it can be served in such large portions.

I had thought of her often—at night, quietly—but I had never imagined running into Rosemary Walton again.

The unknown territory of a day spent together at a friend's wedding, I didn't know what to say to Tommy about her—it would certainly have given him ammo for another pop at You Know Who.

If it was a pity to miss the insights of a specialist, thoughts of love were flowing in my system. And Tommy was quiet, as he often was, inwardly assembling some thoughts.

The texture and shape of his silences, fascination in that bit of a pint that sits above the rim of glass. The first mouthful, the second and third, the part of a journey where you've made enough progress in order to contemplate the end without fearing it.

—How long do you think we'll leave it till next time? he said.

—I don't like to think about that, I said.

—You don't exist in time? Not like the rest of us.

—Not really, I said. Sorry. Just eternity.

The word slipping so easily out of me.

Sweet bar sounds, cups and saucers tinkling on the air, the barman pausing on his way past us, in case there was anything else Tommy Carmody needed. The drinking day pretty much at its peak.

—Wild, Tommy said. *Fuck*ing wild.

Since this was the one face in the world I had watched the most closely, there was something to be said about not talking any more.

How many times had I noticed his attention directed inwards? Just as it would be when you are sewing or reading, just as it would be when you are alone.

—Where is love then? he said.

—You tell me.

—I will, he said. So you're at this beautiful wedding. 'Forever Young', you're feeling nice feelings after all that and you're talking to the young fella handing out the prawns on skewers, the little bite of something to keep you going, and there's all manner of seafood and young ones in nice dresses, and you're not doing too bad yourself, in a suit someone's made for you, in shoes you went to Portugal for, that you had commissioned, and in that moment, in special Portuguese shoes, your heart is opening and you have the politest amount of the little skewers and you mosey around, howya, howya, and you're not so much eavesdropping as absorbing everything everyone is saying, metabolising it, and you're trying not to butt in, cause you'd rather listen, and learn, and it doesn't escape you that what you hear about love is nothing mad or startling or strange, but that's not what fucking empties you, cause you know you're listening cause you have nothing to say that anyone will want to listen to, cause you don't have a clue what you're talking about. Someone might love you and you don't know why. And all you can be is disappointed in yourself. They may as well *not* love you. You may as well love nobody and have nobody love you. You'd rather be at home on your own. No, you'd rather be in the taxi going home, cause as soon as you get home, you want to get a claw-hammer and remove the floorboards so you can get in under them and pull them in over you, so you never have to hear about love again. You're like a dead fish, and you're under your own floor, and you stink like fuck, and even then you can't escape love, it's more sly and secretive than you are, it's cleverer and more charming than you at your best, faster and more consistent, more patient, and don't underestimate its agility, it comes when you're out, and it doesn't care who you are or where you are, if you're under the floorboards, or back in the cab and right back here again, why not, it's a familiar circuit so there is no need to be too frantic about it, but there's no point staying at home if there's no love there.

In all my years knowing Tommy, as devoted to him as I am to You Know Who, I had him down as someone who had worked his way nimbly through the sadnesses. Now it was coming out of him, like knotweed.

The day was going to have its shape—we were going to disappear into the wedding, so I wanted him to know that I'd missed him, and that I thought about him all time, hoping he was doing well.

I did that, I said it, but in a forlorn rather than a friendly way. When there is so much to say, you end up saying nothing very well.

—I'm good, I promise, he said. Just having a moment. This, today, is everything I want, and I can't have it.

—You have love.

—Don't, he said. Look, I'll shake a leg for a bit. I'll be back when the meal is out of the way. We'll have a dance.

The pint he finished in one mouthful looked so delicious, but when he left, I did wonder if I'd ever see him again.

There was not much I would have said about Tommy to Father Ambrose.

It's not that I was planning to disappoint the abbot, it's not that I feared disappointing him. It's that I was curious about what might happen if I did.

If the abbot was known for anything, apart from his

learning, and the sure and deft delivery of a homily, it was for his forbearance. He was a patient man—most monks are—but you'd see him at his most patient on the rare occasion when a situation might get out of hand.

There had been some people living rough in the forest next to the monastery. Travelling folk musicians who didn't do much moving around or play much music. You could hear them play occasionally, with an insistence that existed to mock the delicacy of our singing (we do try our best not to sound like cows).

Sometimes they'd break into the guesthouse or try to steal from the shop and Ambrose would have to go and deal with them, and he'd do this in the most forthright, gentle and effective way.

Never once did he look frightened.

Afterwards, when he'd retrieved the stolen articles, he might say something like, we all have choices to make, and the choices made by our friends in the trees have made life more difficult for them than for us.

Whenever I heard him say that I was sure Ambrose was talking to me.

It may have seemed like he gave no thought to you at all, but over time you'd feel him turning you over, your observance, your obedience, your whatever.

After my first journey to the monastery, I did not leave the property for another three years, but on account of my unusual arrival, on foot, in the rain, unannounced, Ambrose persisted in calling me his wandering monk.

On the day before I left for Dublin, I'd asked him if he was worried that I'd leave for good.

That wasn't a worry for him, Ambrose said, but was it a worry for me?

The question was followed with a reminder that I always had a place at the abbey and that I had never seemed like someone who was passing through. The abbot did not want me to get big-headed, but the brethren were exceptionally fond of me and, in their ways, had come to depend on me.

For what? I think I said.

For *what*? I think Ambrose said.

I was asked to use the journey to consider what the brothers might need me for. For his part, he was happy to let me know that he would be greatly saddened if I did not find my way home again.

When I got back to my room, sure enough there was a message on the voicemail.

It said: to my wandering monk, I have heard good reports of how it went this morning. Well done. You can tell us all about it when you get back. There are new guests, some South Americans, booked in for Monday. This is Saturday. Have a think about what you might like to cook for them.

It was a day and a weekend of rowdy singing and beautiful singing.

Rory was settling into the role of statesman of love.

Anyone within firing range had something lovely sung into their face.

Dinner was bedlam. But why does eating alone, even at a busy wedding reception, even in a refectory full of monks, thrill me as much as anything else in life?

I can't think of one thing—I really can't—that ever meant more to me than the silent meals in the company of the other brothers, my brothers, whom I loved so dearly.

To be content in your own company—and in the company of You Know Who— to be alone, and to know why, and if not to know why, not to think too much about it and, then, no matter what is on your mind, to go alone to your room, to the great silence, and prayer, which is the life you have chosen for yourself.

You do choose it, don't you?

If it was a day for feelings and daydreams, I was giving some thought to what I'd do with the new potatoes I'd make for the South Americans. Brother Gabriel might be persuaded to part with some of his broad beans.

So it wasn't unusual, at Rory and Nuala's wedding, to be imagining myself back in the refectory—lunch was the reward for our devotion—with my brothers sitting either side of me, some of us in from an hour of wheelbarrowing manure, or strimming along the lanes, everyone wolfing their food, and grateful for the seat and the company while one of us went to the pulpit before the words of the scripture twirled through the air like pound notes thrown into a gale.

Most of all I liked it when it was Ambrose's turn to

cook and serve; and I'll admit to a thrill in being waited on by the abbot.

That hour, if it was an hour, where—aprons on, smocks on—we had taken turns in preparing for and clearing up after one another, pushing the trolley, doling out the pudding that everyone ate lots of without any question, listening, giving thanks, not so much for a break in the day but that the day had this shape, and we had journeyed out in it, and now we were on our way back, safe in the knowledge that there were no apples like your own apples, not too bitter not too sweet, and there was no one to thank for this preciousness other than You Know Who.

Rosemary was on a table with her old school hockey team and—this was interesting—she made a detour across the room.

—Permission to approach, she said.

—Permission granted, I said.

—Should I genuflect?

—A curtsy will do, thank you.

Her cheeks and forehead were alight. I took this to be the good workings of the vascular system.

—Were you watching me there? she said.

—Was I?

—You were looking at me like I'm the dessert.

Given why we were all there, I thought she and I might share what was on our minds. We had never been at the point where we were able to ask the question: was there ever anything between us? Is there?

—Well, I'm happy to see you, I said.

—We don't have to be so polite, she said.

—We don't, but I am going to be.

What could someone like me say about desire? I would have been willing to say that I'd reached a point of no return with it. And I'd never felt more like I'd stolen something—from You Know Who—than when Rosemary began telling me of the weekend she'd just spent with her friends at some lake in Mayo.

Barbecuing, picking strawberries, swimming.

Her skin—I may as well tell you about a beautiful sky or warm water; no, some feelings don't get as far as the notebook.

—Were you nervous to see me this morning? she said.

—Probably, yeah, probably. I was just trying to show how cool I am about everything.

—I'm not cool, she said.

Her breath blew sweet and warm on my face. I was conscious of a colour growing in me.

—I'm definitely not cool, I said.

—I know, she said.

Rosemary was a little puzzled when I told her I had to go, I didn't mean to sound rude, but I really had to go.

The Horseshoe Bar was off-limits for wedding folk; a place for the hotel regulars demoted for the day of celebration, or for those made lonesome by it. One of the reasons I'd been steering clear was I'd be sure of finding Tommy there.

He was alone, and in the company of a man dressed as a circus lion-tamer, a resident of the hotel (when the hotel still had those). They weren't directed towards one another or talking, or not talking, but the lion-tamer and Tommy were acquainted in the way of passengers on a long flight.

Everything about the picture was charged by the passing of the years that I'd missed in Tommy's company.

A few pints, needs attended to, repeat.

—Just getting my head together, he said.

He'd been home, and this was as close as Tommy ever came to looking wholesome.

The suit was gone, and he'd showered and put on an old Levi jacket. There was a bandana, too, and a t-shirt hand painted with the words 'Once it was a lie, now it's the truth'. The artist had been in the bar the night before, he said.

Dublin, then, was a city living in praise of itself.

Everyone had an agent, everyone lived on toasted sandwiches. Keen to let the whole world know how unphased they were by the whole world being so enamoured with them. You could be drinking side by side with one of U2, and some old woman with lice. Platinum Amexes, Guinness farts, and now and again, in dirtier bars than this one, someone would sing something to pull the soul out of your body.

—Where's herself? I said.

I was wearing one of my own habits—the stitching wasn't half-bad—and I'd wanted to run into Petra.

I hadn't given much thought to their relationship otherwise. Not what they'd been fighting about, not if they'd get over it, not their future and what there'd be of it.

—Offski, he said.

—Home?

—That's the one place I'd say she hasn't gone. You, Brother Eugene, are the first to know that Mr and Mrs Tommy Carmody the second have parted ways. Look, we're apart most of the time anyway.

—She was there earlier, I said. She was here last night.

—They were her friends in the bar. She was there for them. We do see each other, we did, we have an arrangement to meet up once a week, to argue, to have sex, to talk about her dog. The last time we met to talk about the dog she said she wished I was dead, it's a familiar feeling, I feel the same, and the last time I saw her, this morning, she told me that I was a dead body. A corpse. She wanted to call someone to have it taken away.

—Does she need help? I said. You're obviously not dead.

—She's a person whose opinion I trust more than my own, so if Petra says I'm dead, I must be. When we got home last night, for once we were both there, she took me to her bathroom, we have one each, as you do when you're us, and she pointed to my corpse. She said it needed to be taken away, or she had to get out of there. Are you out of your fucking mind? I said, although the question does make a certain amount of sense, I certainly wouldn't want to brush my teeth in the same place as a decomposing body. So I can see why she has to go, but I didn't want to leave her alone with it, me, so to speak, so we went to bed, fucked like alley cats, vicious, and lovely, and we still had to come along today, cause we'd promised, and Croatians don't break promises, they'll break fingers, and crockery, she broke some last night, but they won't break promises. Now she's gone, gone. When it's gone it's gone. You have the scoop. Don't you want a drink?

—I'm not, I said.

—Drinking?

—Not right now.

—Then you'll have your wits about you to get me one. Let's say, a tall, black, pint-shaped drink, and a small, strong, whiskey-flavoured drink.

It was a distance of a few feet, but there was satisfaction in the small ceremony of going up to the bar, getting something, bringing it back, and hoping that the conversation could resume in a different place.

It didn't take much for Tommy to get the picture.

—You're staying here, right?

—I am.

—I spend half my life in these fucking places, and I still get excited by a ten-dollar Toblerone.

Tommy fist-bumped the lion-tamer, took the drinks I'd just delivered and led the way.

It hadn't taken much for the wedding celebrations to consolidate themselves into a five-star epic.

The dancing was taking place upstairs, but for those who admire merriment in all its shapes, another master-shot of the lobby would have displayed three people dancing alone, one of them singing at the wall; spouses hiding from one another; some little nieces getting down to the business of being asleep on the floor; and one young fella, with the Louis Copeland label still on the sleeve of his suit, exercising the ancestral right of the Irish teenager to steal pints.

On our way up past the ballroom, Rory was in the middle of another version of 'Forever Young', while Nuala was explaining the lyrics of a song (lend me some sugar, I am your neighbour) to a none-too-alert grandparent.

The day was as sweet and ardent as they were.

The bed had been turned down for the night. Tommy declined the invitation to recline on it.

He was going through the souvenirs I'd bought for the brothers. Three very flammable leprechauns and some tea towels that might have carried associations of old-time misogyny. Best to offer no explanation.

—Can we do something about the lighting? he said. I'm spoiled from working on sets, there's never a light that doesn't get adjusting. But this is far too fucking crepuscular.

I turned on the lamp beside him. —How's that?

If the mood had been improved upon, he didn't say so.

—I'm bloody drinking on my own here, he said. Can you not have a little altar wine or something?

—I've got some Lucozade in my bag, I said.

—Warm Lucozade, no less. Top yourself up there, ya little divil, and I'll tell you another story.

With a leprechaun in his lap, Tommy told me again how well I'd done earlier.

—Do you know what seeing you on the altar did to me? It used to make me so fucking angry: the smartest, brightest young fella I'd ever fucking come across had lost all of his marbles. Not your fault, my anger, by the way. But I'm mentioning it now cause it's gone. Gone like Petra is gone, and not coming back.

—How does that feel?

—What I'm getting at, if you'd *let* me, is that I'm no longer angry that you're a monk; I might even be a touch envious. I have a very nice time of it for myself, so it's hard to accept being jealous of anyone—then again, according to my wife, I am supposed to be decomposing in a bathroom, so I don't have the run on anyone. It's a pain in the hole, tell you the truth, being dead, or being convinced that you are, which is the same thing, and in that position, it's perfectly normal to look a bit longingly at someone who has it all thought through.

—Hardly, I said.

—Do you think I'm too old? Do you think the abbot would have me?

—I'm sure there's nothing against old people in principle. And you're forty-five? That's nothing.

—Glad I didn't fall at the first hurdle, he said. Let me make my case and you can see if I stand a chance with your man. Perhaps I can take a spin over there and meet him, see what he says to me, see what I have to say to him, if the chance arises.

There was the same warbling in the throat I get when I hear confessions. I said, —There are always other people you can talk to, if you need to.

—If I need what? he said.

—If you're adrift, I said.

—That's the size of it, Tommy said.

Some experiences and conversations people shouldn't have to go through alone, but intimate moments such as these can emphasise the great distance between people.

Some folk with their souls in peril, monks meet them all the time.

Monks know how to listen, and if it's what a soul wants, it rarely takes that much to restore the peace. But some souls resist and Tommy's blackness—containing menace, sadness, just a little lingering mirth—was entirely different from anything I could recognise.

It would be nice to say I found it harmless.

—Maybe you should talk to the abbot, I said.

—He might invite me into the lifeboat, what do you think?

—I don't think it's entirely up to him who gets in that boat, but he might do.

Tommy went on hesitantly, as if reading aloud from a script without wearing his spectacles.

—It's a relief to be talking like this, and it's not just cause Petra has gone. That's been on the cards since day one. We got married in Greece, in a bit of a hurry. That's how it seemed to go, and that's why you and your dad weren't invited, no one we knew was there. I only proposed to her cause the salads got boring. The same ingredients every day, lots of different ways to cut up a tomato. We wrote our own vows. Private stuff, if you don't mind. You might think this was romantic, and it was, but every single night of our marriage, I could feel You Know Who coming through the wall to remind me that I didn't deserve to be there. And that keeps you limber: he's a good director, he gets the performance out of you. And it worked, how many of these vows did we break? Kept them all. And fucking eejits that we were, we asked the mayor if he could marry us in the afternoon, when the whole place was shuttered up, snoozing. No one else there apart from a few old lads in flip-flops wanting to sell us ice-pops. We had ice-pops to celebrate our wedding. Our lips are bright red and orange in the photo. And it was a very harsh light in that photo, not a romantic light. That was down to the time of the day. Had we been aesthetically and posterity-minded, we could have got married at golden hour.

—The light might have been more crepuscular, I said.

—Crepuscular!

—Monastery light.

—Slanting light.

—Slower light.

—It's taking its own sweet time, he said. I've felt silly even thinking about it, and I've gone mad thinking about it, and now here I am talking about it. It doesn't seem real until you do.

—I'll talk about anything, I said.

—I don't really know where to start, we could go all night.

—I have all night, I said.

—It's a long way from being a corpse in a bath, right? It's not even a spiritual thing, I don't know what it is, Jaysuz I don't have the language. The abbot won't listen to a minute of this, he'll think I'm a madman. Connection, I just want to have some connection to a place. That feeling of being completely at one with yourself, I'm describing it like I know what I'm talking about, but I've never felt anything like it. Connection, I'm trained in it, I can perform it, I feel I know everything about connection without knowing it. I might be setting myself up for a hiding, but maybe that's what I need, more of a humiliation than I've had from Petra. It's that or blow my own head off.

Tommy let that one sit, and I kept quiet, too.

It was like we were stuck there waiting for someone to arrive.

When I first got to the monastery, I'd hear sounds at night. At first it was weeping, then birds nesting and squawking, then sex sounds so loud that someone could have been trying to break through the thin walls in the guesthouse.

It doesn't matter what is said about it being made in the brain, fear is real, and Tommy had every right to be scared. I was scared for him, and I know now that I was angry with him, too, for not being happier, and for not leading the way like he used to do.

If Tommy Carmody couldn't figure it all out, who could?

—Dum-de-dum, he said. Too much?

—A little, I said.

—It'll be my undoing.

—You don't have to be so hard on yourself, I said. You're going very deep very quickly.

It's no magic trick to disappear while being present, and Tommy's transmutation went on.

—I might drown, he said. So, what I'm saying is, Petra is right, I am a dead man, and I want to be alive, I want to get myself together enough to be alive, and only last night I was wondering who I could talk to, and who sashays in but the young monk? I thought, I'll get Brother Eugene's take on things. Wise young man, the wise young man will unstick me, and here I am, nought to fucking sixty, declaring my vocation. Would you listen to me? I agree with Petra, oh me oh my do I agree, she's had to look at me these past few years, she knows what she sees. What do I see? I took a slash there a minute ago, in your very nice bathroom, and I didn't have to take Petra's word for it, but I'm not a dead man. I see myself in the bath and I'm alive, and I don't know what you think you look like when you're in the bath,

I recommend it and I don't, but all you are is a child. You're a child in that bath, a child who's been left alone to fend for himself.

The same thought occurs to me so often now that I assume the answer is obvious to all.

—This is a five-star hotel, so everything was on hand but there's something about being handed a towel by your mother without having to go looking for it. I don't want to know the number but count up all the baths and showers in our lives. Who are we? A child? Our mothers? I have the answer, I'm not going to keep you waiting. We are our own mothers. And we're not that. Think about it. We're not ourselves, we're not them. Not the bath, either, not the water, we're the steam.

—Steam?

—We're steam, he said, as though stating the obvious.

The difficult part of it was Tommy looking at me as if I was supposed do something for him, which I was ready to do but couldn't. We could have kept going until daybreak the following day and would have been no closer to a breakthrough.

—I'm scared, he said. I'm very, very scared.

The fear was audible; it was humming to us through the pipes.

And I had something on my mind, too.

Every now and again I'd thought I heard Rosemary's voice in the hall. What I had seen of her today—it was like thumbing through an old diary. I'd felt as if she had talked as if we were trying to remember all the things we had done together, as if our relationship—affair, friendship, it didn't matter—was already under way.

The lobby would still be rammed full of wedding guests, and Rosemary would be among them. This was so, with hand on heart, I could say that I was out on a stroll when I ran into her.

I was practising my hellos.

Tommy said, —Do you mind if I stay the night? I can't face going home. I already asked at reception and they're full.

We were raking the ashes of what had been said, and he was more or less asleep where he was sitting—I don't think he had slept in days.

I tried to persuade him to sleep in the bed, but he wouldn't.

When she answered her door in what she'd been sleeping in, I felt the involuntary part of myself not visited in so very, very long.

Her arms were bare, and I couldn't look at them, for I know now that I saw Rosemary Walton as if she was imaginary and really believed her to be imaginary. That is what drew me to her, the fact that she would not have to be real.

—What are *you* doing here? she said.

I should have done it; I should have answered her. My best bet was to say what was on my mind, that she could turn me over like old wood. But I closed my eyes and made a silly wish.

We would see how it went.

None of it had to be bad.

Rosemary scanned me scanning her room. It was smaller than mine and the windows were open to an alley, and someone was wearing something, sweet and dense and foreign, or maybe it was the green summer smells from Stephen's Green over the way.

—What *are* you doing here? she said.

—It seemed like a good idea ten seconds ago.

Then I said something along the lines of, this is a very important moment for us to take together. I didn't believe we were ready for love. I didn't think I was ready to receive love. Every day is a struggle to let love in.

—Is that one of your monk parables? she said.

—It probably is.

—I'd have let you come in without any of that. Are you here to stay the night?

—It's already quite late, I said.

—It still counts.

If she was quiet now, she said, if it seemed as if she was indifferent to me being there, it was only cause she was tired after the day.

She wanted to know about when I was going back, where I would be living, what I would be doing.

It was early summer, I said, and the guesthouse would be full of the people Ambrose had promised me, and I would be wiping their toothpaste-splatter off the mirror, and spending most of my time outdoors.

The monastery's farm had hills within hills, and

streams with the most complicated turns in them. The valley there ran from east to west, you could follow the sun; there was enough daylight to keep you thinking too much of anything. She might visit, she said, September, if she did, would be just in time for the best of the apples.

I let her go first and I could tell from the way we kissed that she would let me have my way.

I could be who I was, and I could leave.

We undressed and it was nice the way Rosemary took my clothes from me to hang them up by the window, the spooky shapes they made. She nestled into me, her breathing becoming even and deep as we kissed, and generous in the way that it guided mine.

She was lying on her bed, and she was naked, which meant I must have been, too, which was what was supposed to happen, and all this must have taken a few minutes and I'd no idea what had gone on in that time.

We were barely awake, and in the darkness, we were making love, silently, not to avoid disturbing the people next door but ourselves.

What Rosemary was thinking, I don't know, but when she took my hand I noticed that it was shaking, and I was shy that she was able to see this, on my first time making love, as it was, and that wasn't worth dwelling on for longer than I had to, and maybe I was considering getting out of there, but she held my hand so that it stopped shaking and she used it to pull me towards her—making it clear that I was going about things in an awful hurry, as if there was someplace else I had to be—and to let me know that we were in this moment together, a nice reminder at the right time, since her skin was so unlike anything I'd felt before, and I don't know why I noticed this, but it was a nice temperature, the whole arrangement was like warm cream, and if you like that kind of thing you really do like it, and I had all this heat inside me, and you can kiss that away, to an extent, there was nothing going on other than kissing, and it's nigh on madness to try and recall what else happened, and in what order. It wasn't as if I was taking notes for later.

But I'm seeing us now: we were lying together, lying together in a bed, in a hotel bed, which was unimportant other than it was holding us up, and together, and that's how we were now, with her hair hanging over my chest, and we were moving without having to wonder too much about it, my chest was by hers, I think, beside her or on her, and quietly and intently, we were moving towards something, we were dissolving, if bodies can do that, and we were separate from each other only to the extent that music is apart from the air it floats on, and in that same way that everything can be still and everything can be moving, I didn't dare come and it was good that I didn't, cause the throaty noises she made, at first I didn't know if they were motions of approval or recommendations for adjustment, but when I settled in and listened, the notes were moving upwards just as her spine was making its strange shapes, her chin was thrown up and out, the movements were so even, musical almost, that I was thinking we'd gone as far as we could, and Rosemary stayed that way for a while before her back bent a little more and her face moved back so that all I saw was the tautness of her neck and the underside of her chin, what a sight that was, if we couldn't stay that way for ever it felt like we could, and we did exist in for ever for just a while.

Out of nowhere she whispered, —Say sorry.

And, with eyes right open into hers, that's what I said.

—Say it again, she said. Let me hear it.

—I'm glad that happened with you, I said.

—Shush, she said.

It was a while before we moved; the best part was that Rosemary was trying to catch her breath and couldn't.

I needed to go to the bathroom, but I knew that to leave her arms now would be to lose myself to a dawn that may have had further pleasures in store, but nothing in it would compare to the way in which her face had brightened, in stages, like a sunrise.

The night could be a murky time, but the discoveries that came at vigils were worth treasuring.

Could we have known what good we were doing, if any?

Or did we rise in the night to remind ourselves of defeat?

Despair could be expressed as a boast, and you could get too comfortable in it. Occasionally I sensed these notes in myself and in us all.

Sometimes it ran off like rain, but sadness could settle, day could break, and you'd hardly know it, you were so full of mourning that you were grateful for even the touch of ice or the lavishness of fresh snow.

The room was sweltering. It would have been an idea to get out into some of that greenness. A walk with some-one beautiful and kind on Stephen's Green in the early morning.

She was asleep, not a peep out of her, and I settled into the nice thoughts that, even by being asleep, Rosemary Walton would pull a person out of the gloom of themselves.

And what would you have to say in return?

A kiss would have been nice.

I was going to do that, but instead of waking her up, and with a small measure of my wits about me, I opened a drawer and found a Bible, and thumbing through the pages, I felt that real love was still out of reach, and would stay that way, just where I liked it.

You Know Who knows the meaning of love, the colour of love, and should you want any more than that, You Know Who knows all there is to know about love.

You can have faith in love and still feel like you've been sold a pup, like you've been had. And then I thought, faith in love, where is it, where is my faith in love? You Know Who can prove it but, if you need proof, you don't know love.

*

This was a morning of blue light on grey roofs. I went back to my room in my bare feet. Forgiveness of some kind from the thick carpet.

I didn't know what else to take from it.

If Tommy was up and could talk, and he wanted to talk, we would talk. But he was in bed and fast asleep with his mouth hung open.

My flight was in the early afternoon, and I planned to pack up and go. I went in and out of the bathroom. Either my hands were shaking, or it was very slippery soap.

I had a quick bath and there was no betting against me having another one. The day was coming in around the curtains and I sat in the quiet room with its odours of sheets and sleep. The sheets were in knots and now the morning was letting out its innocent, yellow light.

When Tommy awoke, his yawn was quite melodious. It felt like we'd done something we shouldn't have.

He was looking at me a little sheepishly. In all our time together, we had never spoken like we had the night before. He said, —I was going to say I never could have imagined this. But I could have.

—Was this the first time you've talked like that? I said.

—Did you mind hearing it? he said.

—I haven't said that.

—Don't worry about it, okay?

—Too late, I said. I'm your friend. That's the way it is, I'm going to worry.

—You need to worry about yourself, he said.

I wasn't worried that he would do something to

himself, but I was starting to notice details it didn't help to notice. I was used to him having the shakes; now I had to help him tie the bandana that had seemed so dashing the day before.

He couldn't do his own laces.

If it's hard to say now it was hard to see, then.

And feeling like I had seen Tommy Carmody naked, and perhaps that I had been seen naked, we got up to go.

The best I could do was seem hungry for breakfast. He mightn't have agreed with me, but I felt this morning, and this moment was being sent as a reminder that it was never too late to rejoin the flow of life.

As soon as we got downstairs, he started walking in circles. I don't know what we looked like, but my guess was we had come dressed as ourselves (off-duty monk; actor, probably resting).

It wasn't lost on me that I had slept with Rosemary, but it was over Tommy that I was considering missing my flight. While I dealt with checking out, he exchanged some bon mots with one of the doormen (actor; aspiring). They had such a rapport that Tommy returned with such a bright, inquisitive look that could only mean one thing: he may have been going crazy but he was far too attached to his own reflection to have any intention of talking to the abbot.

He was signing an autograph for a guest, topping it off with a little self-portrait in which he looked more portly and cheerful than he'd looked in a while. Then a nicely pitched monologue about how actors much prefer other people's versions of themselves to their own.

Other people's things. Their stuff.

Tommy used to say this whenever a pint of Guinness was set down in front of him. Nothing so lovely as a pint you hadn't drunk from. As soon as you had, there was nothing so lovely as another person's pint.

I offered to get him one for breakfast, but the barman had read our minds. One got delivered on a tray, and Tommy made very short work of it.

Self-portraits, someone else's Guinness, your own Guinness, I understood it as much as I understood why Tommy was acting like our conversation the night before hadn't happened.

Anyway, he'd alighted on a new idea.

When she left, Petra had broken a vase; the only ornament in the room she was sleeping in, as a matter of fact, but it was an accident, Tommy said, and the vase had to be repaired, and he knew just the woman who could do it.

The studio wasn't far from the Shelbourne. Momoko was a Japanese woman married to the first husband of Tommy's first wife, Niamh.

Hanging from the ceiling in the studio, and all but dominating everything else in it, was a mobile sculpture made of imaginary flags dripping in ceramic egg yolks.

Tommy was completely quiet, moving around below it like someone casing a bank for a robbery.

He was very keyed up about the fact that Momoko used real gold dust in her work. Her materials came from Kyoto—she came from Kyoto—and the vase would be threaded with thin golden lines that would tell a story of Tommy's marriage.

Momoko was an artist—this was a gallery, and she was not in the habit of taking repairs—but Tommy Carmody lived in a world where such requests got granted. She said she'd do the job, and he was given a date to drop in the vase. It would take her a month or two to mend it.

There was a shelf of bowls, decorative, I suppose, but they had me thinking of breakfast cereal, and the nice chat I could have had with Momoko about the ones the monks drink from; how the monks pass a bowl of water from place to place, washing up where they sit, wiping and drying and putting away for the meals to come.

There was a bowl made from dark wood. Walnut, Momoko said.

When I asked her the price, Tommy announced that it was taken care of. She wrapped it in thin paper, and thicker noisier paper, put the bowl in a box that she tied with rope before it went in a bag bigger than the suitcase I'd brought with me.

It was handed to me at the same time as receiving a high-five from Tommy.

—Hey man, he said.

—Hey man, I said.

Our voices sounded so loud, but if we were back to taking things lightly, he was still a worry to me. Once upon a time, I'd believed that his way of seeing the world would be mine for ever. But the things you think you'll worry about are not the things you end up worrying about at all.

(I don't have the bowl any more, but I used it for years.)

—Back to the Shelbo? Tommy said. I'm destroyed from last night.

There was still time to catch my flight.

Every morning Tommy Carmody was the man crawling out of a shipwreck. Good news, I'm alive—this is how I'd remember him, the man who couldn't believe his own luck, and who wanted to be congratulated for being alive.

All you could do was pretend that you too had nothing to lose.

It would be September when Tommy was back here, just as the monks would be preparing for the best of the apples from the orchards.

On the day Tommy picked up the vase, I would be back in my favourite part of the orchard, long and narrow, sloping up from the monastery to the big green field that fed into the forest. Doubtless I'd cut quite a lonely figure, but in the eerie mornings between vigil and lauds, with the fog rising, no one worked more quietly or carefully.

I'd pray for him while I worked, and occasionally I would see him, coming out from the trees, looking wild, or dishevelled in some fine costume from a film or a play, it didn't matter.

I can't say why he came to me in such clear pictures,

and I can't say why they disappeared so soon afterwards.

He was in every psalm.

He was nowhere at all.

You Know When

2019

I'll finish late in the studio today. A client is coming for a first fitting tomorrow, and I'm chalking out the cloth before cutting out the trousers on a suit from a roll of Prince of Wales flannel.

It's quite the imposing pattern. When the client asked if I thought he could pull it off, my pause was an attempt to summon Tommy. The little silences that used to come, the kind of quiet that came from somewhere deeper than I ever had access to.

After the funeral, his wife sent me a courier package with a pair of Tommy's old suits—a chalk-striped one and a linen one.

It was a year or two before I took them apart to make a pattern and the few orders a month for these suits keeps me going quite nicely. Sometimes people will ask to try on the original, but I prefer it to stay on the dummy, tucked away from the sun that hits here in the late afternoons; usually when I have gone home for the day.

Some days I am so low that the air hurts, time hurts. The nights, being closer to death, are sweeter.

This is the normal run of things.

I've begun the jacket of the Prince of Wales suit.

Everyone admires the soft shoulders in the original, and I make my own pads from thin cotton wadding. Nothing too showy. The detailing around the collar will help it sit well on the neck, but my favourite job is to fix the sleeves. The armhole should be high, and the sleeve-head needs to be full enough for the arm to move freely.

You should be able to drink a pint in this suit.

Do the sign of the cross.

Play the guitar.

Do a shift on a building site.

Grow a moustache, shoot a crossbow in a film about musketeers.

Endless ridiculousness.

I should get on. There is never any hurry, but everything in these trousers—the pleats, pockets, fly and linings—needs to be in place by the morning. I go to the dummy to check the waistband on Tommy's suit. Every few weeks, I'll see how things are with it, if it needs sponging or pressing, or if the cloth looks bruised.

I look after it; it's all I have of him.

*

They do this every year around this time, but a few years ago, one day early in May, the brethren took their annual trip to the beach.

Some of us would change in the huts, others shed their habits directly onto the sand. While the others got into their shorts, I was laying out the picnic, my heart rising at the sight of all those pale men inching themselves into the sea, some as still as stone, others moving so timidly as to barely corrugate the water.

Did it matter that I was being left behind? The way a pet might be left alone when the family went off on holiday.

We took turns, as we did at the monastery, to cook and serve and clean up. As the Tupperware and urns of tea were being set into the sand, there was the off-kilter sight of the outsize figure of Brother Michael Anthony exiting one of the huts to walk, almost dizzily, to the water.

He was much older than any of us, so much larger, but frail and timid now as never before. The water was up to his thighs, and he could barely lift his arms to balance himself.

I had no business being judgemental, but I'd been surprised to see him make the trip at all. He was rarely found in the chapel anymore; we might occasionally find him in the refectory at lunch.

If Michael Anthony had not been one of us for a while, he was one of us today. Skin ghostly white, white hair translucent, was he ninety years old or more, a hundred?

Only Peter, the young novitiate, was galloping friskily

into the waves. Michael Anthony was paying no mind to the fact that someone was swooping around him like a gull.

Peter was just happy to be out and about. A long winter that had passed straight through spring. A day at the beach had been called for.

The brethren were merely doing what people did in summer—enjoying an activity that was supposed to take you away from the daily grind. Even if we'd never wanted our lives to be anything other than work and prayer, it was a lovely thing for a May morning to be reminded that we belonged to You Know Who, but You Know Who didn't belong to us.

Michael Anthony was standing the other way, looking past me up the beach towards the huts.

He was waving or dragging one hand through the water. If he was trying to communicate a message to me it hadn't got through, and without much sense of ceremony at all he fell backwards into the water.

Ambrose was an army man, and he got the old man upright, holding him under the oxters to drag him out of the water.

Peter called out, —He's going to die, he's going to die!

I was in up to my knees, managing to fall into the water just as Ambrose got his cargo ashore.

Michael Anthony was convulsing very gently as we laid him on the sand. We got him wrapped in some towels and laid his robes and habit gently over him. He was even paler than before. But no one had a phone to try for an ambulance, and no one knew what to do.

We were waiting to be told what to do.

His mouth might have twitched.

Ambrose attempted to resuscitate him. I was trying to find the pulse.

He was dead and had probably died in the water.

I knelt to kiss the old man's face. I could smell his breakfast.

Someone put a towel over him, and Ambrose took a few steps back to indicate that we should do the same.

We may have prayed.

We turned to see Peter run along the beach with a cart borrowed from one of the burger vans on the esplanade. Soon we were all moving, but this was not the impressive assemblage of brethren you'd normally see sweeping in and out of the chapel. Only Peter was going at speed, operating at such high intensity that we may have tried to help but he got the body onto the trolley all by himself.

He managed to get halfway up the beach, he was almost there, before the wheels sank into the sand.

I was trying to ignore the fact that he was grunting and getting angry. Poor man, Peter was sure he'd frightened his brother to death.

He was wrong, but however much we tried to spell it out, and however much we tried to dig the wheels out of the sand, the more it became clear that, even if there was an ambulance on the way, not to get Michael Anthony out of here by ourselves felt like a betrayal.

It's not enough to say we were defeated, that isn't it.

All we'd had of Michael Anthony had been taken away by the waves.

When an energy leaves that you know can't be replaced, I don't understand how that works. I've tried but there is no way of describing the feeling when you see someone go and you feel that you've let them go.

My habit was soaking wet and everyone looked so cold.

Once we'd watched the body be carried off by paramedics, Ambrose said that we should continue with our food.

Peter was against it, but he was reminded that it would be a year before there was another picnic. Everyone got changed, and we ate the rolls, and I made sure everyone had tea the way they liked it.

We were all so gaunt and pale, and I truly cannot remember what we said, or if we spoke, so it was not that different from any other meal. Monks know what to do with their faces, and I must have pressed my expression into one of concern and repose.

If I can't say that anyone cried, this was not a feeling of release that we read about in St Paul to the Thessalonians.

Pure, upright and blameless.

It didn't even enter my mind that we had given our brother back to the thin air from where he'd come.

Many times, on the journey home to the monastery, I wanted to say something in tribute to Michael Anthony. If others were going through what I was going through, it was pointless to speak to people who were trying so hard to listen to themselves.

It was just another way of saying that we were all scared.

I was washing the Tupperware we'd taken to the beach when I got a message that the abbot wanted to see me in his study.

—There was a message from your father on the machine, he said. He says you're to call him immediately. But I need to keep the line free to speak to Michael Anthony's family. You are permitted to call tomorrow after lunch.

I will say that Ambrose said this very softly. He permitted me time to consider my response.

—Thank you, Father, I said.

—But it will be my duty to ask you what is being spoken about on your call.

The previous winter, sure that I was about to begin a new life with Rosemary Walton, I had left the monastery for a month or two, probably three.

I'd left a note for Ambrose to say I wasn't coming back.

The message said that perhaps I had given all I could to life as a monk and that perhaps I was not able to give anything more. Much like the boy who didn't want to go to the pictures, and who didn't know how to behave at the Debs, this was all a bit directionless.

I wondered, now, if I had chosen to be with Rosemary

Walton to foreshorten the process of choosing love over You Know Who. When I'd returned to the monastery, Ambrose did ask if I had a clearer sense of what love was, and what it meant to love You Know Who as much as the world.

As much as, not more than, he'd said.

I told him why I'd left (I needed to know love) and why I'd come back (I still needed to), and Ambrose asked me repeatedly if there was anywhere else I needed to be.

I told him I didn't know.

All this had been said through a mist of tears that he didn't acknowledge.

Wasn't it a pity I didn't spend the time away coming up with some answers?

It would have been easier to list the pleasures of a lovely month in a cosy cottage in Stoneybatter.

Rosemary Walton and I had had what we had.

Sometimes, in her bedroom in the morning, when she was pottering around doing something lovely and sustaining, I was more sure of her future than my own. It was a position I was growing ever more comfortable in, and from which I took all the comfort I could, even in the face of the obvious, which was that I had always seen love as a trophy.

Once I'd won it, did I know what to do with it?

I really did that—think of Rosemary Walton like a prize.

What kind of prize?

Someone with eyes shining the moment they opened in the morning. Someone with the conviction that other people were more interesting than they were. Just the fact of getting to be called her boyfriend was a source of delight.

I was supposed to be looking for work. There was no good way to do it; I was going around having meetings with my old professors, and the days soon became heavy with indecision and worry.

Mine, that I was better off being a social worker than a GP.

Hers, that I would not manage to find anything at all.

We'd talk, fuck, sleep.

I'd walk, pray, cook, clean, do her laundry, darn her old things.

The caring for each other. People did do that; reach the accessible part of themselves, find it and give it to someone.

Then the weight of expectation passed into exhaustion.

One day Rosemary came home from work to find me filling the freezer with Bolognese, enough there for a week of meals. The batch cooking wasn't unusual (monks like a meal plan) but she was worried I was leaving.

Why would I leave? I'd said.

Cause you've been preparing to go since the day you arrived, she'd said.

Non-stop: labelling the Tupperware; scraping at the

grout in the bathroom; buying new napkins and folding them the way I'd do in mass; hours, perhaps a full day, filing all her old bank statements.

All in the attempt to leave her life better off than I had found it.

This was when Rosemary suggested it might be it for us. All of which I was wondering about now, with Michael Anthony's last breath still in my nostrils, and replaying the montage of a bunch of sad monks eating a picnic on a beach after a young Slovakian priest had nigh-on scared an old man to death.

—I sense you're pining for something, Ambrose said. Or you're adjusting. The effort is rather enveloping you.

—It's been a sad day, I said.

—Not today. You look eternally pensive, like you are uncomfortable in your surroundings.

—I feel like I'm in the right place, Father.

—Do you? he said.

Better to think of other things; of opening the door to Rosemary when she got back from work in the evening. I'd lift her up and swing her round and round so that she'd catch her breath sharply enough to make a note that swooped through the air.

This sound still makes its way to wherever I am and it cuts through me now, a note at the beginning of a hymn. It is one of those bright, clean, bottomless things, with nothing in it that isn't pure, and it's audible now, coming off the walls of the room where I'm writing. Around the room it goes, into my belly and up through my chest to colour my cheeks.

To Ambrose, I said, —I belong here. I belong to you and my brothers.

—Do you? he said. Do you. Today was a sad day. What did it make you feel?

—I'm not sure I have the words, Father.

—You do. Today was evidence that Michael Anthony died as he lived, surrounded by love. We had him to ourselves for long enough. Now he is in the arms of the Lord.

Before getting on with his calls to Michael Anthony's family, Ambrose said I should prepare the soul for chapel, and life was to carry on. We were all going to go in much the same way as Michael Anthony had.

I don't know where in the Bible it says that if we don't believe we can survive everything, we will survive anything, but I took this revelation with me to sleep that night. And in the morning, at vigils, with the chapel coloured in a rich, almost tropical way, I sensed the brethren singing like never before.

Would you have known that we had lost one of our own (so carefully were we observing every syllable and turn in a line)?

When I think about it now, isn't that one reason to pray?

For what reason other than grief, for what reason other than despair, for what reason other than relief, for what reason other than joy, and how this was all part of You Know Who's plan for us.

Some days you just have to sing, and it's likely I have not sung that way since.

Father Ambrose was listening in from an armchair as I made the call.

—I wasn't going to get in touch, Dad said. I'm not on for a chat. Tommy asked me to call. He's having a birthday do. A select few. You made the cut, Ian.

He still called me Ian, I still called him Dad.

We had not been talking. The fault was mine, and it was his and that account will never be settled.

—I'm honoured, I said.

—You should be, Dad said. Tommy loves you.

—I love him. But I don't know if that will be possible. I don't go to parties. We don't do that, Dad.

—It's a sixtieth.

—Even so, I said.

—Don't make this difficult, Ian. You're going to want to come. Talk to your boss, tell him you need another sabbatical. I think you'll find him agreeable to the idea.

—Is anything the matter? I said.

—Apart from the fact that I got interrogated by a priest for wanting to speak to my own son? Tommy's had some health stuff, but he's through it now. How about you? Things have been a little tense, I imagine, since you've been recaptured.

—Maybe we can ease off on that kind of talk, I said. And I'm not sure I'll be able to leave here.

—I'm sorry to say this, Ian, but you've run away before.

He signed off with that.

My guess is that I would apologise, and Dad would too, if we knew what we're doing it for. When I was staying with Rosemary, he'd told me—helpfully, since everything parents do is under the guise of being helpful—that he didn't recognise me any more.

I may have replied that the same could have been said in return.

Ambrose took a seat so that we were facing the windows to the quadrangle, where our little automated lawnmower was making its rounds.

When I first arrived at the monastery, he'd been very curious about my family. Lately, less so, but now he asked why I never spoke to my father about my life.

I have had plenty of time to consider whether my mother's faith led to mine. If she had been alive, we would very likely have ended up on a walk, being reflective, probably in the monastery's orchard, having conversations about all our certainties. She had not been, and I was not, resigned to death being the end, and yet, I was and wasn't sure that I would ever encounter my mother again.

If it was uncertain, I didn't want it to be *that* uncertain.

—What are your plans? Ambrose said.

—I don't know, I said. But I do have a question for you.

—The questions you've been asking lately are giving the Lord a run for his money. I spoke to your father last night. Do you have a plan for what might occur if you do go to see your friend?

—I don't think I do, I said.

—No plans, no forethought?

—I have no plans other than being here. I'm supposed to be here.

—Do you feel lost? Ambrose said.

—I am lost, I said.

—As much as I would like for you to be on a different path, he said, you might say that being lost out there is the same as being lost in here.

I'd seen Tommy almost exactly a year or so before this, around Easter.

Holy week is the most precious time in the monastery's calendar, and it was one of those mornings which don't come along very often, sharply coloured, and with the potential for the soul taking flight.

Have you ever imagined what it's like to be a monk?

It's so hard to describe that I prefer to let people use their imaginations anyway.

If I feel people might listen for a minute, I tell them how much I used to enjoy saying mass, an hour or two in which we can float, or sometimes fly altogether.

I was preparing myself for duty, finding the spirit ready. Perhaps it had even been waiting for me. And when Brother Gabriel, the doorkeeper for the week, led us into the chapel, I was almost expecting to see someone standing in the front row.

Visitors participate in services from the aisles in the naves. There are murals and carvings and the most vivid glass and in spring the chapel takes on a kind of party light.

Tommy, naturally, had found the good angle.

The colours coalescing into a picture of health.

Beside him was a woman I didn't know, tall, dark and handsome, and quite young, who had to be a part of if not responsible for the painting of that picture. He was bundled up in a coat he probably wore on film sets, smiling over at me as if I should have expected to see him there, which I had.

Tommy once asked me about the story with You Know Who.

The story, what is it? No gist, no story, I said. There must be, he said.

The gist with You Know Who is this: you put on your worst clothes to have your best thoughts.

The gist with You Know Who is like a good winter coat. You don't wear it every day, but it's always there. You Know Who exists in every bowl of soup, and each mouthful.

The gist is that it lasts for ever.

The gist is You Know Who makes mean men soft: he makes them glorious.

The gist with You Know Who involves there being nothing there, and that there will be adjustments to the nothing, qualifications to the impossible. The gist with You Know Who is that all this guarantees immortality and the gist with You Know Who is that none of it is up to you.

The brethren weren't supposed to hang around too long after services. When I hung back after we had all walked out of the chapel, my hug with Tommy didn't happen in the way I thought it might.

Automatically, in a brotherly way.

I could feel him deciding to just as I was deciding to.

And I'm only mentioning it to remind myself that I ever hugged Tommy Carmody (and it comes back to me a lot now).

The conversation was as casual as the introduction to his fiancée.

We shared some nice words about the woollen mills Elaine had wanted to visit on their trip to the Highlands, which was a last-minute thing, otherwise Tommy would have written to let me know they were coming.

In the days that followed, I saw as much of them as if they were on retreat. No sign of them first thing in the morning, but I could count on seeing them at mass and then later at vespers and compline. I don't know if they could pick out mine from the other voices emanating from the altar, but I'd sing so hopefully during each service, all the more pious for having Tommy Carmody there to witness it.

The sound of his voice, audible from the nave, was unmistakable as the flavour of the milk and butter you grew up with.

One afternoon, as I was ironing the sheets for the altar, Tommy came to the room next to the laundry. He knew from my letters that's where I'd be.

I kept the place as clean as a dairy.

If I was ironing tablecloths, I enjoyed it as much as my near-enough carnal pleasure in the smells there—steam and soap. But Tommy smelled differently than I remembered; of her, and of them, I had to suppose.

Tommy's career on the screen—charismatic gargoyle—and his journey through love weren't intertwined, but if you'd looked at his life as closely as I had, the idea of him being in love, marrying, being married, whatever, stoked a fire I was no longer aware of in myself.

That I could not identify or explain it is the reason you are reading these words (I am trying to explain it to myself). Often it was as simple as dealing with my inner heat, even though I would convince myself it was something else. And I had convinced myself that my thoughts towards Tommy and any of his lovers were generous ones.

Tommy had left Elaine reading on a bench in the garden.

I heard how moved she was by her visit here, by the richness of our voices, even the silences before and after the monks sang.

It seemed right to respond to this compliment with an extended silence. There we stood like fellow laundry workers, folding sheets in two and four and eight.

When everything that could be was stacked and put away, Tommy went to see if Elaine was all right (she was).

He asked if we could take a walk.

While I wasn't quite finished with the laundry, I led him around by the orchard and the barley fields. Tommy thought the hills here were like messy, unfinished versions of the hills in a painting.

We headed into the forest, and I was better on the paths than he was.

It hadn't been half an hour, but he was missing Elaine. He wanted to be down there, in their bed, their bodies a contour in the skyline, the hills folding like limbs around them.

He put his hand around my shoulder just to let me know this was a walk like any other. Two friends out in the world, getting all there was to get from it.

As it turns out, he was here to ask me something.

There were still cobwebs of fog on the trees, the sun glowing obligingly through them as he said, —This one's for good.

—Glad to hear it, I said.

—The mad thing is, I didn't think we'd anything in common. She was in the production office of the last film, one of the accountants. Normally I swing by the offices to say hello to everyone then fuck off out of there, but they give us these per diems, it's like you're being paid twice, and they come in a brown envelope, so you've got some nice walking-around money. And there'd be little handwritten notes in mine. Love hearts and stars and all that. After a while, I'd be opening up the envelope and throwing away the cash just to get to the note. Funny little things, mad stuff, a bit loolah, I was thinking. But I'm a goner, Eugene, I'm an absolute goner.

When I'd been his lodger, in those first weeks out of school, emerging towards adulthood, I took on Tommy's love stories as something close to my own. My attachment to his attachments.

—She's an absolute smasher, I said.

—I'm glad you think so. I wasn't going to put you on the spot. Or I am, but not about that. I suppose you've twigged that I'm up to something. The mad head on me, sneaking up there to help you with the laundry. I'm in a stupor half the time. Mush. The head is gone. But that's what I'm marrying. We're making plans, and plans for plans.

Dublin could get a bit much from time to time, he said. And he'd been spending some time back at Crouch End and was thinking they'd move there.

We spoke of our first summer together, moments which hardly seemed to matter when we were in them. All these years further on, there was nothing in particular to wish for; not for time to stay where it was, but perhaps for one more chance to hang around like this, talking shite, as we were certainly doing.

But there were quite a few jobs needing to be done before vespers.

I was about to tell Tommy I had to get back to it when he said, —We'd like you to do the wedding. Vows, bow and nod and smile, what have you.

I mumbled something like, lovely, wow, lovely, I'm honoured.

—I'd have to get permission, I said. We can't just go booking flights.

—Who do you ask, the abbot? Can I speak to him? I'm very persuasive.

—I don't think that would go down well, I said.

—But you'll ask, he said.

On the way down, at each turn in the path, I stopped and made a wish.

That evening after supper, Ambrose asked me if I'd had a good conversation with my friend and if there was anything I wanted to say, and the answer was no.

In vigils the next morning, with all the brethren's love and concern for the world wafting up with the candle-smoke, the thought of presiding over Tommy's wedding started a pummelling feeling in my chest that left me too exhausted to sing or to pray or to do much other than sit and stare.

They would be asleep somewhere nearby, and I prayed for Tommy and Elaine. But the light of morning was slow in making its presence felt.

The dullness of the tiles in the chapel, and the meagreness of the grout, was felt as a reproach.

The real worry was that I couldn't bear to be around love.

Tommy and Elaine had theirs; later, all it took was a following glance at them leaving mass for a walk in the orchard, where the rapt way he listened to her indicated that I'd be better off not being so fearful for someone who was not fearful for himself.

After lunch, I went to the door of the abbot's study, as I said I would do.

There was some outgoing mail in the tray, empty milk drums waiting to be cut up to hold seedlings, the hiking boots Ambrose wore for the walk up the hill to the bees. Monks like us cared for the things we cared for, in the best way that we could; we loved what we loved, and sometimes life threw all that into the wind.

Standing there, trying to find the words.

I was imagining a wedding; okay, I'd done plenty of those, I was imagining Tommy's wedding; okay, I was happy for him, I was imagining Tommy's wedding to Elaine; okay, I was very happy for them.

Someone else's love was still proof of the existence of it.

Plenty of love to be going on with elsewhere, thank you very much—in the sky, in the apples, in folding laundry.

How clever of love to get itself everywhere.

And no matter how long I would stand there, trying to find good words to ask for something I didn't want to do, I wouldn't find them.

So I didn't knock on the door, and I didn't ask.

And this is why I was quite satisfied with letting Tommy think that the abbot was not giving me permission to travel to their wedding.

Tommy Carmody was always a light that required a little finding. But there are many sorts of light in the world.

The chapel's candles, candlelight, I could go on about candlelight.

Strip-lights in the monastery kitchen.

Light can be desolate, suggestive, generous or harsh.

Dashboard lights, tail-lights.

Bare skin makes light. It glistens and can reflect light in a way that can make you feel quite immortal.

There are those guiding lights, then.

The lights of love, trembling light, a lingering light you only see in the small hours, when you catch yourself hoping, and at which point You Know Who might slip out of the shadows. Will he sneak a glance at you?

The Longwood hotel was going to be full of friends gathering for the birthday dinner, and Tommy would happen to be among them.

The bedroom had the same old carpet smell as the guesthouse at the monastery, and I felt quite at home there. Just as I was closing the curtains to prepare for a nap, a taxi pulled up and Elaine got out. She seemed a bit tired and fretful, and when she went to the passenger door, and she let him out of the car, I think I thought this was Daniel Day Lewis but more fragile than that, like an elderly royal.

Tommy was not doing a very good job of getting out of the car without looking lost and lonely, and very sick.

I'm not sure they spoke; I'm not sure he looked strong enough to.

While being outwitted by the shoulder strap on his bag, Tommy gave a halting look up to where I was, without seeing me, I don't think, and without knowing that I had caught a glimpse of a dying man.

The dining room was art directed in its richness. When I saw Dad was having one, too, I had a pint of Guinness, and we waited for the others.

Someone had arranged the lighting to soothe and cajole us into behaving like this was just another dinner, and, when people floated down from their rooms, we could have been in a village meeting, or in a hastily assembled committee.

One or two well-known faces.

The family of Scottish actors I'd met before. One of them was as half-famous as Tommy, a Martin somebody; and his brothers, or cousins, all of whom often got parts in the same drama as their better-known family member.

We did our best with the cocktails Elaine organised, sipping neatly and wandering around.

A few minutes of that, puppets being led by strings.

Weren't we all there to celebrate Tommy? We were, we were, it was just a matter of believing it.

Dinner was at a long table, like the refectory at the monastery.

Someone had papered the dining room with stills from Tommy's films, and I went to look for one of *The Golden Rooftops*; the Carmody of the floppy hair and the linen suits. There he was standing on a bridge, in the right kind of sunset, and the light in the dining room was pink and green, and people's faces were glowing with nervousness, or the end of the first drink.

On any other night I would have been happy for the chance to talk over a few drinks. That this was not really a birthday party was not a topic to get stuck on.

And bang, Tommy was there in the room.

The skin on his face was as puffy as a padded envelope. But the suit was a double-breasted jacket in 10 oz navy chalk-stripe.

Ten-ounce woollen cloth, upper out-ticket pocket.

He ignored the seat kept for him at the top of the table.

Dinner was served. I wasn't hungry; no one was.

The night was washing past us all.

Elaine came and went from time to time, and I was calling on You Know Who and for the grace to let them be as she helped Tommy eat.

Something was going to happen that I could have no control over; I had no idea what that would be, and Dad, who was drinking more than I was, asked me why I was going so fast. But each place had several glasses at it, people drinking wine with their pints, some of us with shorts, too, mirroring the glass of whiskey that Tommy carried with him but wasn't drinking from.

Every time I looked up he'd moved to a different place, one further away from where I was sitting. Eventually he came to sit by me but not close enough so that I could hear what he was saying without moving towards him, which I didn't want to do.

I knew to give him a moment. There was nothing that unusual about this; you had to observe your minute's silence in the presence of Tommy Carmody.

The lapel of his suit. Peaked, with a slanted buttonhole.

—You don't see much of that any more, I said.

—Better believe it, he said.

—How is everything? I said.

—I forget, he said.

I was draining one of the glasses in front of me and wondering how much of the poise he was displaying was practised and how much was involuntary. An actor can draw a scene towards them by making a noise or a spectacle, or by being silent, and that silence draws everything in the space towards them.

What were his intentions? I didn't know.

Now I can say that he wanted our company, but he didn't want our attention.

—Shouldn't we start behaving like people at a party? he said.

Meanwhile, I was trying to say thank you to him. The kind of feeble gratitude you express as you steal the last seat on the lifeboat. Just once I wanted to get it out right. I did try, and Tommy turned his head away as my sentences became more ramshackle.

The thank yous had only caused his face to shine with pain and soon they were abandoned.

He turned his gaze to the glass he wasn't drinking from. I don't think he took a single sip from it all evening.

Dinner—being here, eating, being still alive—had left him faint.

It looked like he was about to slide under the table and only fear of the consequences prevented me from asking him to sit up straight.

Elaine was helping Tommy with dessert (a half-destroyed trifle). When it became clear that he had finished, she did what a lover, or a parent, would do: she began eating from his bowl.

What I should not say, what I am ashamed to say, is that it took the sight of him being so vulnerable before it occurred to me, before I allowed it to. That's what it took, and he would never know—that I could only recognise my love for him in juxtaposition with suffering and loss.

Then Dad appeared and decided we were all going to have some wine he'd chosen.

Dad wasn't even sure we would like the wine, but for reasons best known to himself, he had been determined to order it. This was so, with hand on heart, we could all say that it was just another evening.

Tommy's fingers were so fine around the whiskey tumbler.

He'd put it down, just out of reach, pursing his lips at my father's account of the spellbinding wines made from chenin blanc grown on schist soils.

He tried the wine, then Dad did, and I did.

Perhaps the flavours were distorted by distraction and nerves; at first it was like drinking a boozy, bitter candle.

Dad couldn't tell what Tommy thought of it. He asked but Tommy didn't answer.

—People say it's a difficult wine, Dad said.

Tommy extended his hand towards a glass and then let it tremble in the air. With all the old richness still in voice, he said, —We're difficult people.

When Tommy asked if I wanted to take a turn around the garden with him before bed, I almost said no. Something was going to be said between us—it turns out that a lot was said—and I wasn't sure I wanted to be in that conversation.

At first it was a simple moment of two old friends sitting on a bench in a garden of louche and lanky rose bushes.

This was the location.

Through the window was another art-directed scene; the drawing room had been staged for a late night of music. Tommy's old Martin acoustic was resting against a sofa. Occasionally Elaine would come to beckon us inside, and one of the lesser Scottish cousins came to the window to moon at us. The theatrical type.

This was the scene.

Another element is thirty years of friendship.

The additional element is loss, an experience you think you can understand in its entirety. But one abandonment (grief, betrayal, loneliness) is not transferable to another.

—Maybe we'll take a walk in the morning? I said.

—Unlikely, Tommy said.

—All this? I said, gesticulating at not very much.

—Are you wondering why I didn't tell you about being ill?

—No one else said a thing either.

—I asked them not to, he said.

—Why?

—I didn't want you worrying for me.

If I've been lonely for him since, this was one of the loneliest moments of all. The only thing as desolate as this moment is a chapel in the hours before a dawn you are not ready for.

—Is that us then? I said, sounding like I was winding up a meeting.

His look said one thing: maybe we want to try all this again?

He said, —Making your acquaintance was quite the surprise, if you don't mind me saying. All those years ago.

—All those years ago, I said.

—How long are you at this monk thing now? he said.

—Twenty years, I said. Give or take.

—You can ask me for my sins if you like?

—Wouldn't do that to you, I said.

—What if I asked to confess something?

—Confession? I said. I'm not sure.

Knowing Tommy was going to die—he'd have another six weeks—was like looking in a mirror and finding no reflection.

—Bless me Father, for I have sinned, he said.

—Really? I said.

—Fucking *really*, he said.

I summoned the spirit as best as I could, as quickly as I could, said a prayer and we began.

—It is forty-five years since my last confession, he said.

—Okay, I said.

—Have we begun?

—We have.

—If I'm going to pack it all in, I'll have to do a fair bit of summarising. You'd be tucked up in the bed and I'd only be getting to 1986. I'll focus on one or two highlights. I want to talk about a certain summer. I don't think there's been a summer like it. It's all golden now. The weather was like a fucking melody following us around. And I'd grown so fond of you that I'd been starting to worry every time you went out to work on the building site. That you'd get into a fight with one of the labourers or be run over by a digger. Only when it was just us, sitting in the garden, I felt like I was properly looking after you. I promised your Dad I'd do that.

By coming outside to sit with me and engaging me in

a conversation he wasn't strong enough for, Tommy was, I think, showing me a kind of kindness that I was not prepared for, and which has proved everlasting.

—You never met Niamh, he said. But the night we went to the gig in Kentish Town, you knew there was something wrong with me. I told you why. She was there when she wasn't. I was scared that I'd told you too much—it's a lot, other people's ghosts—but the next morning, when you came in for your cereal, the eggs I made you, very nice, and you were making a packed lunch. The big block of cheese that was your prized possession. Would I like a sandwich? you said. You asked me that every time. And I could see you were ready to be off, and I was sorry to see you go, there wouldn't have been many hellos and goodbyes between us, it was a come and go kind of thing, but I was so worried about you going, and I couldn't say this—bats in the belfry—but I was sure this was the last time I'd ever see you alive. I wasn't so comfortable with that, if you get me. And you had your lunchbox and your backpack, and it was like I was seeing you off to school. Did I stand in the porch? I don't know, but I do know that I was sure that being around me was going to be very bad for you. I was certain that if I didn't remove myself some kind of harm was going to come your way.

To anyone observing us, we may have looked like we were having an argument.

There is no feeling as awful as sensing the person you care the most about being unable to hear you tell them you might not be able for what they have to say to you.

He said, —It's completely nuts to say it, but I was seeing your dead body on the path. And I went into my room, and I packed the bag I used to take with me on shoots, I made sure I had enough for a week on the road. Like, I was dying to get into the bed, but about twenty minutes after you went out, I was following you down the path. The only reason I wasn't seeing your corpse was that I felt sure that I was making things better by going. And the head did get quieter the moment I was out of there. When I saw you a month or two later, I was still all over the shop. The headspace took a long time in coming. So, when I came to see you in the monastery, I was hanging on to the terrible notion that I'd done something wrong.

If only I could have released Tommy and Tommy could have released me. Take us back to a time when we were strangers, me to him, him to me.

He was easier to love, and easier to get on with, when he was dying.

It made you wonder if he had ever not been, if we had ever known another way of being.

He said, —And when I saw you saying mass, fair dues to her, Elaine noticed it, or she noticed something, and as we were having our sandwiches in the little graveyard, she had an umbrella for us, and she put it up even though it wasn't quite raining—it was and it wasn't raining—and she put it up and she asked me what was the matter, and I still don't know why I did this, but I went off to take a piss in the bushes, well I do know why, the waterworks are a little unreliable with all this stuff going on with me, and when I came back from my piss I was bawling crying, and Elaine, the poor thing, was confused but she was also calm cause she knew I wasn't upset with her, and she wasn't being pushy but she wanted to know, and she was still holding the umbrella, and I tried to go back to my sandwich, but none of that had anything to do with why I was so fucking sad, and why the feeling had been sitting there like a big brick, and I thought crying would be the end of it, but I couldn't stop, even though I thought it was all out of me, and Elaine had put the umbrella away by this stage, and she was eating my sandwich, she does that, and I knew what I was about to say was going to sound strange to her, cause it was all quite a long time ago, but it wasn't that strange at all, cause she'd seen how moved I was watching you sing in the church, and she was moved, too, she likes a bit of pageantry, and I said, all right, I'll tell you.

That Tommy should have been preoccupied with settling his account was only too obvious. He was nervous, too. I didn't think so at the time, but he had to have been.

He said, —I was acting like she was dragging this thing out of me, when all along I'd been dying to talk about it, and I was up off the bench by this point, half thinking I could go back into the chapel to find you, kill two birds with one stone, cause this is sort of about you, Eugene, if you haven't already guessed, and it's more about you than you know, cause I think of you all the time and various times over the years I've wanted to call you up and talk about it, and I always put it away, cause it couldn't be about that, it couldn't be about that day you went off to work and when you came home to an empty house.

—You went to rehab, I said. You told me.

—I did, I did. I should have moved in for good. All the messing caught up with me in the end, the big, stupid head on me, and I did sort of know you were all right, you were probably much more all right than I thought.

—I was, I said.

—It's not that I ever stopped noticing you or caring about you. I did notice, I did care.

—I was okay, Tommy, I was okay.

—I thought you wouldn't be. I thought I had to go. And then you invited me for dinner.

—I did.

—And I didn't come, he said.

—No, I said.

—I let people down, he said. I do. This was coming so long that I am glad it got there when it did.

—This is a terrible thing to be carrying, I said.

Once you behold someone in the way that I'd beheld him that night, there is no release from it. I didn't assign him any penance, and Tommy—did I see him gliding?—walked back to the door to tell Elaine he'd be another few minutes.

I called after him, but he didn't hear me. I wanted to say something to make him feel better, I wanted him to know that the wine had tasted like trifle.

*

The drawing room smelled of the garden in the evening: warm ground, and tequila.

The tale of Tommy's time on a film in Morocco was making its way around us. He'd hired a car on a day off and had been having a few illicit goes at the duty-free on the way and pulled in to have a sleep in the shade, and when he woke up there was a hen in the passenger seat, laying an egg. He took the egg home and had it for breakfast.

Everyone found it hilarious.

Tommy was just the kind of guy stories stuck to. And a new energy was finding its way through him. Everyone we knew was here, he said, and since that was the case, why didn't we make more of a night of it?

Good idea?

Bad idea?

Yes, and yes.

Tommy picked up the guitar and, before anyone knew it, it was two-three-four in the morning, and like roosters crowing Tommy and his friends were singing of Texas dust and true believers and being home again home again, home.

They could have kept doing this, could have kept playing and singing, through the night into the next day if need be.

But it took a while before I joined in.

Singing a favourite song or an old hymn is like taking a walk around your own memories.

It is like being able to talk in a dream.

In church, in the bath, on the bus, I'd always found

that any kind of singing does you good. The way you sing may be a response to all that's before you, but the moment will be held in a different kind of reality.

This one said Tommy Carmody didn't belong to me, he belonged to all of us there, and oh how his life should have been longer, so there'd be more of him to go around.

I've since seen photos of that night. Glasses full, glasses empty, one of the Scottish cousins looking unwell, it doesn't matter.

Elaine is here, there and everywhere.

And there's one of her and Tommy.

In the photo his eyes are fixed on her and on somewhere beyond the camera, and the end of his own life. The day Tommy had asked me to do their wedding, he'd said he was a goner, and the picture confirms this. They were newly married and in love, and in many ways, there is no point in thinking about anything else.

Never a self-effacing man, I can't believe Tommy would have wanted to disappear from life when he did. He would have tried to argue death away, or ignore it. I believe what Tommy Carmody wanted from the end of his life was not to avoid the deadly and tireless silences, but to be ready when they came.

I still wonder if he was as ready as he seemed that night.

Whether or not he felt he was—I was not.

The photo says, what's to be done with love but hold on to what you can get of it?

*

With everyone off to bed for an hour or two, and with some nice light being thrown from the fireplace and the candles, Tommy asked if we could take a spin outside before bed.

The dawn appeared on cue, the wrong blue against a perfect blue, outbuildings against sky. With the plants sitting in fresh sunlight, I pointed out enough wild lamb's lettuce on the lawn to plan an omelette.

What did we talk about next?

The refreshing breakfast tea you could make with mint and nettles, chicory and dandelions. The sweetness of spotting the wandering sheep controlling the grass, which meant I could point out the flowers controlling the pests, the leafhoppers and mantises and ladybirds. The worms which looked so cute but did so much damage to the leaves.

We had to talk about something.

Had he ever found his way towards You Know Who?

We had just come very close.

In our way of rubbing along together, there was a faith bigger than all of our memories and apologies and breakfasts, which had been there all along, and which allowed for forgiveness but was more than it, and which couldn't really be contained within the word friendship.

—I could see about some breakfast for you, I said.

—Not quite there yet, Tommy said.

I went to get us some coffee. The sigh he gave when I handed over the cup said, there is more, but we have talked about all we are going to talk about.

These are now some of my favourite daydreams—the garden insane with colours emerging from inside other colours. The force with which I can imagine those plants shining and, with them, the very principle of summer being removed from my life.

Were we this garden, were we this scene?

Whenever I recall it, I tell the artist—time—to go back and start again.

More of the green, more of the red, less of the yellow.

One day in April, Father Ambrose drove into town to find me in the emergency room.

The musicians who'd been living wild in the woods above the monastery; one of them—Davy was his name: hairy, riding something of a high, genial until he wasn't—had come into the gift shop and, like a milkman there to collect his empties, taken the old safe from under our noses.

He didn't seem to be very concerned that I was pursuing him through the orchard. In a way, it was just bad timing that I caught up with him just as he reached the polytunnels.

Davy had to think about it when I asked him what he was doing with the safe (which may have held all of twenty pounds in coins).

He pointed towards the forest as though the trees needed the money.

Was it a matter of self-defence that he came at me with a spade?

I did think for a moment that he was going to beat me to death with it.

He looked at the spade, and at me, in something like disbelief, and I wondered if he said to himself: oh no, not this again. He threw the spade into an apple tree and ran off in the most peculiar zigzag.

Perhaps Davy didn't believe himself to have a bad bone in his body, perhaps he felt this was in self-defence, but Ambrose wasn't interested in any of this. He wanted to know why a monk would debase himself in anger.

I wanted him to understand that I was trying to protect what was ours.

Wasn't that what all the brethren did (and do)?

We protect, and we protect, and we protect.

Then—and I can still not make sense of the when and why—Ambrose let me know that Tommy had died.

I've not gone back to Longwood since then, but I have looked at pictures of the garden where we sat. The roses are out, the bench is patiently waiting for life-defining experiences that probably won't occur, and Tommy isn't there, and I am not there.

In another life, I may have asked Ambrose why he waited before telling me.

Or I may have asked the young doctor who was

stitching me up to stop what he was doing for a moment. But the cut made by the spade needed seeing to and I felt useless without something to do.

I was, of course, doing my best to bleach the moment of any significance, which is why—concentrating not on what had been but what was about to be—I asked Ambrose if we should go up to the forest in the morning to talk with Davy and his friends.

Ambrose didn't think we should.

And for a man like him, delaying the news about Tommy must have made perfect sense.

If you are not fully of this life, it is not that momentous when someone leaves it (Ambrose did think of it this way, I know).

It is the religious man's way of living with the unliveable.

It was not the thought of never seeing Tommy again. In ways I was already resigned to that and, having called Elaine in the days prior, I was grateful that his pain was over.

It was the details of his life—plans, journeys, promises, mistakes. The nights in Crouch End spent preposterously dancing, Tommy barking moves like a cheerful general. The hospital, where his widow would now be dazedly pacing.

My doctor was finished with me.

Paracetamol, tetanus, pat on the head.

Before driving us back to the monastery, Ambrose suggested a detour.

—It won't be strictly legitimate monastic behaviour, he said.

I was wondering if Ambrose came for fish and chips whenever he was in town (which was more often than the rest of us).

If it was different from walking around London with a certain someone thirty years ago, attachments change in the most unpredictable ways and regardless of the way he'd told me about Tommy's death, I'd rather have been in no other company.

Could I have known that Tommy Carmody would die young?

Could I have known that the abbot would be the one to tell me?

Could I have known that it would be the night I'd decide to leave the brethren? Could I have known that I'd not say so for a very long time?

Did I know that the monks would always be my friends? That they would always be my brothers, and this was an open-hearted place, one that I'd be sad to be leave?

The questions line up so neatly now, as though one thought follows obediently from another, which they rarely do.

We ate the food off the bonnet of the car. The chips that came with the fish were newly fried and very hot and Ambrose was so starving that he burned his mouth on them.

—I remember your friend when he came to visit last year, he said. He had a very nice time with us, as I recall, a good look around, too. I think he found us in good shape. You're sad, aren't you?

—I am, Father. Do I seem it?

—It's not my place to tell you what you should be, he said.

He took a sachet of ketchup and bit it open and folded it neatly enough to tell me he did this a lot. As still happens so often, I pictured Tommy in the summer we met.

Trying to lose weight after that film in France, he'd had the idea to give up eating carbs. The staff in the local café were coached on his preferences for sandwiches with no bread. What looked to me like a very big pile of bacon and avocado was in fact a sandwich with no bread.

None of this would have been interesting—an actor prepares, etc. etc.—but things can occur and then only start to make sense years later. Does the fact of thinking about the way a person wants their sandwich mean that you loved them, and you still do?

In the weeks since his birthday party (where almost no one had wished him happy birthday), I'd stopped thinking about Tommy in the way that I used to. His death was an end to worrying about how I'd ever keep up with him in conversation. No more being the slow one or the quiet one, or the one who couldn't believe that Tommy Carmody would ever have been his friend, who couldn't believe that luck.

Ambrose said grace, by which I mean that I stood by the car with my chips and cried.

—This is a very important time for you, he said.

The decision to travel to Tommy's funeral would be mine to make, he said. There would be funds and free time put at my disposal.

—Thank you, Father, I said.

—It's one of the many good things a monk can do, he said. These people come to us, and we process, and we pray, and we give all we have to them, thinking not of ourselves. Nothing we have belongs to us: even the fields, the flagstones, the glass in those windows is for others. I spoke to a woman the other day. She comes on retreat, and she does a very thorough job in the garden. You'll find some visitors go through the motions, but she really turns over the soil. It's like having an army of new earthworms. I'd never seen anything other than overly tended herbaceous borders to suggest something was the matter. As we were leaving mass, she asked for confession. But I was rather on a high, as you can imagine; it had been one of the better homilies, and she said she could come back later. Something told me that if I let her go, she wouldn't come back. I invited her to take a seat by the guesthouse, and I went to make her a cup of something. Not normal service, offering catering.

Ambrose was right. So often it felt like we were living in a visitor centre rather than a monastery.

—I sat with her, and held on to the tea, which she hadn't wanted. She was very pale indeed, the colour of the walls, if I'm allowed to imbue the moment with a little lyricism, and she was ready to talk. We took a walk into the garden so that we would have more privacy, muggins here carrying the cup all this time, and before the gate was closed, she told me she didn't want to be alive any more, and that she didn't want to confess this as a sin. In fact, this was a realisation she was quite proud of. She had it all planned, a bridge nearby, she'd mapped it out, she'd gone as far as planning a picnic, can you believe? She was even going to make a little cake. What I should have added is that she'd stopped crying by this point. She was being all very clear, but she was speaking very faintly, so I had to ask her to repeat it. She was planning to commit suicide that afternoon, and she was going to go up there, and would I help? Would I help her? I said I would even though I didn't know what she meant. She asked if I'd hold her hand, and the next moment we were holding hands rather tightly, and I knew that by keeping her hand in mine, well, not that I was doing much other than being there, and I'd like to keep you in that moment, if I may. Her face was changing. She's a lovely looking woman—monks *are* allowed to notice these things—and her face was recovering its rightful colour, and the blood seemed to be in the right place. This was happening before my eyes, and I wondered if I could stand up and lead her out of there, and everyone would move on with their day, I had some beeswax to attend to, but she became very interested in the bench we were sitting on, and everything around it, the new leaves on the trees, she thought they were like little bits of salad. We stayed where we were, and we said nothing, and I reciprocated. Often it's all we can do, provide a peaceful mirror for people. There were people coming and going by this stage, Brother Christopher was on his way to the work-shed, and our Christopher is not the type of fellow to pass without a wave or hello, and the little interruption was all this poor woman needed. And I suggested a walk and Christopher came up trumps with lots of chat about in-hand stone carving. It certainly is a very interesting activity, one slip and you're out. The woman was fascinated, it was a nice diversion, I think, and then we walked very sweetly and nicely to the car, and I drove her to the hospital, just where I found you.

When we'd both finished eating, Ambrose folded up his greasy paper, asked for me for mine, and with eyes closed said a prayer as we did at the end of every meal.

We'd missed the final service of the day yet I was enfolded by the sweet and solemn hymns that would have been sung by my brothers.

At the end of a day, the chapel took on a dreaminess few ever get to see. The place shimmering with candle-light was our reward for another day of devotion.

Ambrose double-checked the altar arrangement for vigils and everything else in the morning. The thin-mouthedness of men at worship is all very familiar to me, but so much of what is good in the world—the generous, the steadfast, the curious—is provided by the likes of this man.

When he prayed, he would tilt his face slightly, like a dog enjoying a breeze. Now he was off, the internal melody taking on its own form and life.

Nowadays, that picture of us kneeling side by side, quietly worrying for the soul of Tommy Carmody, arrives like a message from some sweet world I may never actually have lived in. And those summer days in Crouch End come to me like time borrowed from someone else's existence.

Which Tommy was I praying for?

London, Dublin or now?

At his birthday dinner, Elaine was cutting and arranging his food so that every bite would be alike.

Something to do with his diet, she said. And Tommy, eating in a grisly, delicate way, was alert to all that was going on—and not much was going on other than everyone at the party was trying not to stare at him, in this world of his own, timing his mouthfuls, counting the number of chews he took.

When it came down to it, we all had the same thing in common.

The most interesting man everyone knew was going to die soon.

And, when Tommy lost count of his chews, he'd stop and start again.

*

Dublin, then. And the Shelbourne, where no one gave a second look at the monk at the top of the lobby stairs.

I wasn't alone in thinking to commemorate Tommy there, and the atmosphere in the hotel was more akin to the day of a big match, an All-Ireland or a rugby international. The other guests seemed to know the drill. Two young women on their way down from breakfast caught me looking their way.

A murmur to each other before, completely in sync, raising their handbags in salute.

This must have been how it was for state funerals.

From there it was two or three minutes to the church.

I walked smartly across Stephen's Green, weaving past other funeral-goers—no one I knew very well, and all tied up with the business of their own hearts—and I wondered how anyone was managing to put one foot in front of another, and how we were going to get through the morning.

All around the church was outrageously busy.

I pushed to the front of the queue, but no one else was doing that. Was it more cheerful than a funeral was supposed to be or was it that many of us had cried our tears the night before?

The wake had been bursting in ways that we'd all half-hope for.

I'd been of the opinion that nothing was going to touch me any more than the news of Tommy's death, but there was something so natural about people popping in to a restaurant on the South Circular Road to reminisce and to give out and catch up, have a moan, have a laugh, all on their way home from work or on their way out.

Was it that they were, as I was, expecting Tommy—probably exasperatedly—to walk into his own wake?

If Dublin was Tommy Carmody, there was even now the sureness of his presence. Any day in the city, even the day of his funeral, was ripe with that possibility.

It would be easier to talk about who wasn't at the wake.

Niamh was somewhere in Germany, and Petra was somewhere across town, and when I spoke to Rosemary Walton, she figured that they'd stayed away out of respect for Elaine.

If his marriages were not a side of Tommy's life that I ever really knew (and I have not tried to represent them here), nobody, I'm sure of it, marries with the idea that it might end.

The certainty is as ridiculous and comforting as You Know Who.

There were plenty of servers, but Elaine was coming and going, backing out from the kitchen with trays, handing out pints. Being in a room full of people who may have known your husband for longer, and differently than you did, I can't imagine a night more baffling and distressing; I can only suppose she was keeping herself busy.

Rosemary was on her way to 'a dinner' and hadn't been able to resist popping in to say hello.

Being in Dublin not that long after living with her—I can't remember how long; your relationship with time changes once you live in a monastery—gave me the impression of never having been away.

If Tommy was still alive (and I did believe that he was), he was going to sidle up and tell us to get on with it.

—He loved you, Rosemary said.

—Do you think?

—You made a fine pair, she said. The actor and the monk.

—What am I going to do without him? I said.

—You know exactly what to do, Rosemary said. You take him with you.

I'd thought there might be music at the wake. Some old fella had been sitting on a chair by the door, keeping himself to himself.

I asked Rosemary who he was, but no one seemed to know.

In it for the long haul, he was already in the suit for the next day, with the shirt sitting up nicely on his neck. The knot on the tie was perfect, but he was very sad-looking and tired looking.

The lights were low, or they'd been turned down, and he loosened the tie. At first, I thought something was the matter, he had an upset stomach or something, but it was his way of getting into the moment, finding the song.

Now 'The Parting Glass' was gently slipping out of him but as it carried on, there was a sense of the singer burning out, using up all his fuel.

Elaine came over with a fresh pint and it got choked right down and, either the drink kicked in or he just had the knack, but the song just lifted itself out of him, like it needed to be sung.

This could have been his routine, Rosemary thought, tour the jurisdiction in search of wakes to sing at. Tonight, he'd almost sung the head off himself, and the singsong continued.

We got there as easily as passing around a jug of water at a meal.

Were we singing Tommy into the past?

Songs can wait till the singer is ready, and sometimes you just have to sing something away. By the end of the night, my chest was battered from it all.

When I went to walk Rosemary to her taxi, people had begun dancing, and the old man was fast asleep in his chair.

I was glad to get back out into the world. The street felt spacious. But Rosemary was regarding me a little oddly.

I did look a little ragged. My shirt was soaked from the crying.

—Love is stupid, Ian. People are stupid for falling in love. I'm stupid.

—I am stupid too.

—Perfect, but please don't be in love now. You've got a funny expression on your face.

—I'm not in love, I said.

—You look a bit puzzled, like you're doing a crossword.

—Tonight's been quite a lot, I said.

Her face was turning from one thought to another. —Do you think we moved in together too soon? When we did.

—I would have done that differently, I said. I would have done a lot differently.

—I know there are no rules. But it feels like we broke a few.

—Heat of the moment? I said.

—Heat of a very weird moment, she said.

Her cab pulled up, and I had an unexpected jolt in the heart to find someone waiting for her in it.

Pedro was in banking, a mover of important money, she said. Exactly the kind of person I could imagine Rosemary being with. Exactly the kind of person she could imagine herself being with. If decency could be bundled up and made portable, he had just enough of it to carry around.

When Rosemary kissed me goodbye and, demented with cheeriness, I waved their taxi off into the night, it was from certainty that love can be a matter of fact.

Love can speak and be spoken.

And it can give you the slip.

But Tommy's wake was still unfolding inside the restaurant.

The little bit of melancholy that came from saying goodbye to Rosemary and her friend made each moment all the more precious and in no time at all I had made it onto the dance floor with everyone, friends and strangers, and while I couldn't move to save my life, there was space for me make my own shapes and move in my own little circles. Pretty okay to keep going as long as the music did, as long as the music wouldn't stop.

I have felt more ecstasy in a church than I have ever let on. Fetching, carrying, following the script, dealing with the possibility that the spirit might at any moment leave the room never to return. You can have a perfectly good day, as a monk, or as anyone, without that spirit in attendance.

By the time Tommy's funeral came around, I had come to the realisation that there was no need to worry, there never would be, and I walked onto the altar with that view on proceedings.

The roof would be listening.

The walls would be waiting.

The ceiling would send those long-ago thoughts.

I'd take the steps I'd taken before.

So I'm going to say that the funeral was just another mass.

It was enough to walk to the lectern to the creak of a pew: the room tuning itself in. I'd been expecting to officiate along with some others, but being asked by Elaine to deliver the eulogy was like being presented with a different exam to the one I'd prepared for.

But this is the clergyman's everyday reality, the expectation that you will leave a moment better off for your presence.

If I have caught anything of Tommy in these pages,

it's partly cause I've had all this spare time to dwell in his company. In his company I can be quiet and wait for his voice to reach me. In that moment, I didn't feel I could sum him up.

I could have spoken about the summer we won't get back, but I couldn't think of just one moment that captured the summer in Crouch End.

I might have sung something.

But no, the spirit came to me just when I needed it.

I started with pad kid poured curd pulled cod.

I said it twice.

I said it ten times.

The tongue-twisters went down as well as could be expected, which is more than could be said for most homilies I've given. The ones in French said: If my uncle shaves your uncle, your uncle will be shaved. If these six sausages are so dry, then these six sausages are dry sausages. People got more in the mood with *ces saucissons-ci sont six sous, ces saucissons-ci sont aussi six sous.*

We were all about ready to go to the butcher's.

Then, someone called out —It all goes so fast, doesn't it? and we all applauded.

As I was finishing up, Elaine signalled to me there was still time for me to say something more, if I wanted to, and something else came to me just before I stepped away from the lectern.

From the altar, I took in everyone here who'd loved Tommy Carmody, and I thought of the ways in which a life can be long and love can be short and a love that has gone can still lift you up in ways that we can't describe, except to go back to the idea of this inner heat that you are only aware of when it leaves.

Love, being the most natural thing in the world, does come and go—before it returns in the way that it came to me now in the very, very clear sense that Tommy was still there with us. Surely, we could differ on the fact of him being dead, or still alive, but the man who'd meant so much to me was not the same and exactly the same person as the man who'd meant so much to them.

And I thought: this is how it will be, he will come and go, the inner heat will fade, but it will return in new forms; the colour in someone's face as they smile at something silly you have said, the warmth in the hand that reaches for yours.

And I thought: love is much more than Tommy and me, and since we all knew he was gone, I did want to say one thing that brought him back, just for a few moments of brightness, so that we could be in his company one last time, insofar as we had ever left it.

And I thought: the moment I step off this altar, into the merriment and bewilderment of the afters, life will be different from before, and it will not be as good.

I said, —There's a story I'd like to tell about Tommy. I know we all have them. And I'm sorry for everyone here. But I'm certain last night and this morning would have met with his approval and I'm sure he would have had no hesitation in walking to the top of the queue outside. And I want to enjoy this moment, in your company, and in his. It's something we might consider, the belief that he's still here.

I had people's attention.

Perhaps they were relieved that someone else was struggling to capture him in something resembling a well-shaped tale.

I wish I had been able to give them one.

I wish I had been able to say that you can know inner heat, and you can learn to live without it, you can find comfort and love (You Know What) and you can lose it (Mum, then Dad, then You Know Who), and a person can come and go and they can mean everything and when they go, life simply empties and you will have no idea how to fill it.

And you won't.

Life will reassemble itself in parts, it will come back to you in langoustines for breakfast, and sandwiches with no bread, and chips eaten off a car bonnet, and if that isn't enough, you keep going until you find something that might mean as much as he does.

It's an admirable thing to be, one who moves through a place with all the belligerent optimism of a westerly.

One who moves others.

Everyone there loved Tommy Carmody.

Dad, in the front row, was very hungover. He was trying to open a bottle of Ballygowan without letting it fizz over.

Maybe there'll be another chance for us. But this is how it was at the wake and the funeral mass: the occasion that most calls for a sign of love is the one time where it doesn't happen. We hadn't spoken since Longwood House, and, if we ever speak again, I would be surprised if we ever mention Tommy, just as we have reassured ourselves by no longer speaking about my mother.

When I closed the door on my mother's room on her last morning, our relationship ended. It didn't live on, and I tried not to think of her. To remember my mother was to acknowledge that she was no longer there.

The moment Dad told me she had died, I remember shaking like a little animal. When he put me to bed, I took his face in my hands and promised that I'd never leave him.

Imagine making a promise like that.

Imagine breaking it.

—There's one occasion I'd like to talk about, I said. When I became a monk, I had the arrogance to assume people would want to be part of my ordination. The pageant part of it. If I was going to be swanning about in robes and kissing a tiled floor, I wanted people to see me. As it happened, I was one of two being ordained, and the church was filled with nice people from the Philippines; how many of them had made the journey I don't know, but there were so many of them that they had to occupy the side of the church reserved for my family. They were all yapping and passing drinks like they were at some barbecue, and it took my mind off the fact that I didn't have anyone, which was how I'd wanted it maybe. But I found myself wishing it was over, this lovely day. The abbot was looking at me to see if I was all right, and I wasn't one bit all right, and he made out like he had business with a candle so that he could come around my end of the altar just so he could get a closer look, and I don't think he liked what he saw at all, the absolute state of me at my own ordination, and I got notification from on high that I was to buck up. But I sidled over to the abbot and asked if they could spare me for five minutes. When he said no, I said I needed to go to the bathroom, and that's not something a person can say no to. Why hadn't I gone beforehand? he said. And I was trying to think why not, and I couldn't cause I didn't need to go at all, and I went outside anyway.

I got the story a bit muddled up here, but I know that I left the chapel right in the middle of my own ordination.

The monastery has a very long driveway and there were people heading down it. This was not the last time I ever saw him, but what came next—the image of Tommy coming up the drive, struggling underneath that bale of hay—still calls on me as our final moment.

He'd seen it was me and I beckoned him on and oh, the sight of him—a man of the cloth is permitted to talk about visions, after all—and Tommy was wearing a linen suit the colour of a pint of Jersey milk.

From the door of the chapel, in my robes, I watched an angel weave towards me.

The bale got heaved at my feet.

By then, I was placing this in a series of moments.

Tommy walking in on me in the glasshouse; Tommy on the floor of his room, staring at his own bed; Tommy in the Horseshoe bar, and at the top of the stairs in the lobby of the Shelbourne. I kept it to that.

He sat down on the bale and patted it for me to join him. Sorry he was late, etcetera, but why in the name of Jaysuz was I outside?

It felt right to say I was feeling a little lost.

—Well, I'm here now, he said.

This wasn't quite the time to be catching up, but I wondered where he'd got the hay and how he'd travelled with it, and if he was going to take it with him afterwards. Don't worry about that, was the answer.

—It's a wonder you didn't bring the acoustic, I said.

—Do you need some accompaniment?

—Aren't our voices enough?

—Well, they'd want to be good, he said.

He asked me if my mind was made up, and I had no idea if it was or not, or how life would be (and best to leave that there), but all it took to make me feel sure of myself was a friend turning up, all it took was him saying, I'm here now.

When I said that I was ready, we walked into the chapel, hand in hand like schoolboys.

The light at that time of day had its part to play, too,

buttery and not too bright, the tones inviting inquiring thoughts: what would I ever have done without him?

There wasn't much space inside, and he asked if he could squeeze into the front row for a good view. I'd seen him at the theatre—Tommy Carmody was not your average spectator—but something in the solemn pottering on the altar must have soothed him.

He mimed crying on a person's shoulder, then just before I was presented to the bishop, he inhaled very deeply, breathing himself into absolute stillness. Then the brothers sang, without which this story would not make sense. As the music passed from our mouths to the sky, more of the mysteries of the day rushed in on me.

The music was travelling through Tommy, too.

How far inside him was it going?

The moment where I lay down on the floor must have been too much for him, and the rest of the ceremony was passed like this, with his eyes closed. When Tommy shook himself awake (yes, he'd been asleep), his chin sank to his chest, hips settling into a slow rotation, like someone balancing themselves on a speeding train. But our expressions are not always what you think, and what he was thinking about I would never know.

I'd love to say it was the sound of my voice that brought the smile to his face.

The brethren sing for hours every day. To stave off the silence settling in too deep around them, they offer up hymns as pure as nothingness. On the occasions when I join them, often I am the only one to hear their music. and still they sing.

Our hearts empty and fill like reservoirs.

A Note on the Author

Andrew Meehan has published five books: *One Star Awake*, *The Mystery of Love*, *Instant Fires* and *Best Friends*. He grew up in Dublin and now lives in Glasgow, where he teaches Creative Writing at the University of Strathclyde.